Books by Richard McDaniel

Matt Dawson Cybernetic Investigations

The Angry Assassin

One Too Many Buffaloes

The Cave Gods

The Devil's Cruise

Historical Novel

In Search of Destiny

For more information go to:

http://www.lulu.com/RichardMcDaniel

The Devil's Cruise

By Richard McDaniel

While every precaution has been taken in the preparation of this book, Lulu Enterprises assumes no responsibilities for errors or omissions, or for damages resulting from the use of information contained herein. The appearance and contents of this book are the sole responsibility of the author.

A Matt Dawson Cybernetic Investigation

One Too Many Buffaloes

One

Clarissa was the last one to arrive. She found a seat in the back. Up front, at the head table, Devin Ashton clanged his spoon against his glass. The whole group had finally assembled for breakfast. A pair of Akepas, little yellow birds, turning this way and that, flew through the dining room and out the open walls to the veranda. The birds passed over the heads of the other hotel guests on their way toward the crashing waves on the beach. The sun was beaming in through the open area, coming up out of the ocean over the other Hawaiian Islands to the east. Devin's wife, sitting to his left squirmed in her chair. They just let the damned birds fly wherever, this had happened several times when they had eaten here, but what surprised her was that no one else seemed to care or even notice.

It just wasn't proper or sanitary.

Devin starred down on his employees with his icy glare. "Now that we're all up and ready to start another busy day of our little holiday on Kauai, I would like to take a minute to be serious. I want to thank all of you for the success of Ashton Ventures -- it's got my name on it, after all -- but it's you and your hard work that have given us a start in this new era. I want to thank Hank particularly. He found Jules Marston and made us stay with his Utel Electronics long enough to get to the IPO. You probably all know by now that we have made an almost embarrassing return on our original investment." Devin turned and led a small round of applause for Hank Fieny seated at one of the tables close to the front.

Devin cleared his throat and continued. "The venture capital business will soon make an important mark on the industrial history of the United States, and we are one of the pioneers. We can be proud of that. If we pick and choose correctly, the new advances which are coming down the pike in computer and integrated circuit technology are going to make business history and make us all richer. Judging from your efforts last year, the eighties are going to be spectacular. So let's give everyone a hand."

The assembled group dutifully gave out a subdued round of applause. Devin reached down for a sip of his orange juice. He allowed his eyes to briefly lock on to those of the woman in the back. Clarissa, an attractive blond, looked down at her napkin, trying to hide a smile, and then tried mightily to stifle a yawn. She had enjoyed the horseback ride on the beach yesterday, but this whole company picnic thing was getting boring. Having to be on guard not to let Amelia see any of the little sexy glances she gave Devin was getting old. Since Amelia was along, Devin wasn't coming within ten feet of her. It was different when she and Devin were alone in his office. Clarissa was one very personal secretary to this chairman of the board. She looked carefully at Devin. Yes, he was a good choice, even if he was graying at the temples. He was what, forty-six now, but he still looked pretty sexy. She wondered how many years she might have left herself, to complete the plan before her looks were gone. *Next May, I'll be thirty-six*, she thought. *Oh God!*

Devin had brought everyone in the company to this lovely hotel in Princeville, Kauai, the Garden Isle. It was beautiful, but you normally don't have to go on a vacation with the people you work with. Devin had brought his entire family, the two boys, Carson and Aaron, and the daughter Beth, the other spoiled brat. They all were a bunch of stuffed shirts.   Devin wasn't that way.   They got it from their

mother, Mrs. Top Drawer.

You could see the beauty of her youth in Amelia Ashton's face. Her hair was grey

now, and cut short, but her warm outward personality belied the true nature below,

or so Devin had told Clarissa. His wife had always been a cold person, limiting her

emotions either happy or sad or amorous. Clarissa took the cue and always lavished

her affections on him, whenever they were alone.

"Today I've hired a special guide for something that I've really been looking

forward to, a hike up the cliffs of Na Pali on the northwest corner of the island. Oh,

that's wrong. Na Pali means "the cliffs". Anyway I hope any of you that want to will

join us. Our guide, Billy Kamauu, is going to give us a brief description of our hike

today. Billy is a pure Hawaiian, a rare thing to be proud of. Billy?"

Billy stood up. As he stood by Devin, he was almost a foot shorter than Devin's

six foot four, but he looked fit and trim, a poster boy for the idealized Hawaiian

surfer.

"Aloha and welcome to Kauai, the home of Mount Waialeale. That's the big

mountain you hear people talk about but you rarely see because of the clouds in the

center of the island. Our Hawaiian gods live up there in those clouds and watch

everything we do.   When this island was formed, great lava flows rose up from the

earth and streamed out into the ocean on the northwest corner of the island, forming

giant cliffs rising two to three thousand feet from the ocean waves. This is Na Pali.

Today we are going to take a short hike down the Kalalau Trail across these black

lava out flows. On the hike we will pass some of the wild taro plants left over from

when my ancestors had little Taro patches on these cliffs. Taro is the plant from

which we make Poi, which we will be serving at the luau tonight along with the

roasted pig. There will also be some pools, in which you may wish to stop and cool

off, so you might want to wear your bathing suits. The trip is not too hard, but I need you all to be careful to stay on the trail, as some parts are extremely high. I hope you all enjoy the trip and again, Aloha," Billy said.

Ha. High, you think that's high, Clarissa thought. Having grown up in Wyoming and done some hiking in the Rocky Mountains, she doubted the heights would bother her, that is, if she decided to go.

Devin stood up again. "OK, after the hike we'll all meet back on my favorite beach in Hawaii, Ke'e, where the Na Pali trail starts, for a luau this evening. Any questions?" asked Devin.

"How long is the hike?" Betty Garrison asked. Betty was the plump little lady who was the head of the accounting department.

"I'm glad someone asked that", Devin's wife Amelia muttered.

"We'll go about six miles, but you can turn back anytime you want," Billy answered.

"Mother, do I have to go?" Beth asked.

Clarissa could tell even from where she sat, that Beth was not into it. Beth was seventeen and not too fond of the outdoors, though she was not a wilting violet, as she did like to play tennis.

"I'm not going, you promised me I could go surfing again today," Aaron said.

"Honestly, Aaron sometimes you act as if you were fifteen going on nine," Amelia said. "Hush both of you. We'll discuss this after breakfast." They were all sitting at the head table. "We don't want anyone to see that the family isn't into the program," she whispered into Beth's ear. Amelia Ashton was a year younger than her husband and came from a well-established San Francisco family. She had gone back east to school at Vassar, and when she married Devin, she brought with her a considerable fortune to combine with his.

Devin was the only son of the owner of one of San Francisco's oldest department stores. His father had sold the stores to one of the big chains and Devin started his business life with a mere twenty million dollars. Amelia had tried to keep her looks,

but as is nature's way she felt she looked a lot older than Devin.

"Devin, I'm not too keen on taking a six-mile hike, or would that be twelve-mile,

if it were six miles just one way?"

Devin ignored the question. "Alright, we'll meet at the jeeps at ten," Devin said

and sat down.

Everyone got up and started to move away from the tables. "Devin, I think Beth

and Aaron and I will pass on the hike," Amelia said.

"Oh come on, Amelia, it's beautiful up there." He looked around for the waiter

and the check he had asked for. "You don't have to go the whole way," Devin said

with a trace of annoyance.

Carson chimed in, "At least I'm looking forward to this, Dad." Carson was twenty-

two and in Stanford law school. He enjoyed everything his father did.

"Beth wants to sunbathe and Aaron wants to surf," Amelia reported.

"Yes, Daddy. Why can't we do what we want?" Beth whined.

"You two can do that at Ke'e. Amelia it's not too strenuous for you, is it? You

walk that far when you play golf."

"If I go I'll be the only one that doesn't go the whole way. I'll be all by myself

when I turn back," Amelia said.

"Let me see what I can do about that." Devin spied Clarisa who as about to leave

the room. "Clarisa, can I see you a minute?"

Clarisa came obediently over to the Aston family group. She tried not to respond

to the smirk on Devin's face. I guess he trying to prove how fearless and brave he is

she thought.

"Are you going on the hike? I'd really appreciate it if you kept Amelia company.

She doesn't plan to go the whole way, and wants someone along in case she turns

back. I hope you don't mind," Devin said.

Clarisa smiled. Yeah and we can compare notes about how good you are in bed she thought.

"That sounds perfect to me. I don't want to go the whole distance either. It will be fun to be your trail partner, Mrs. Ashton," Clarisa said feigning a bright smile.

"Amelia, please, if we are going to be trail partners, you can surely call me Amelia."

"OK, it sounds like this will be a beautiful hike," Clarisa said trying to sound convincing.

"Thanks, Clarisa. See you at ten," Devin said.

Devin had rented seven jeeps to carry everyone and Aaron's surfboard. Billy Kamauu drove the lead jeep with Devin, Beth, and Aaron with his surfboard tied on the top. Carson drove the second jeep, his current girl friend in the right hand seat, with Clarisa sitting beside Amelia in the back. The road up to Princeville was good at first but as they headed on around to the north of the island, the road withered away. They came to a series of one way, fragile looking bridges over the many waterways coming off Mount Waialeale.

"These bridges look as if they have only a limited number of passages left in them," Amelia said.

"I think Hawaiians don't want to have this area fully developed as are some of the other parts of the island. We've already taken too much of their sacred lands from them," Clarisa said.

"You seem to have a high regard for these native people."

"Yes, I do. I spent a few summers working with the Sioux Indians. I have always admired their approach to life. They only take what they need." Amelia noted a strange look in her eyes when Clarisa made this pronouncement.

They rode in silence for a while. Clarisa was thinking what an accident it was that this woman had everything just by being born into the right family and I have had to plan and sweat to get what I need. The time for the next phase of the plan is near.

"Have you enjoyed the island?" Amelia asked.

"It's really beautiful, I particularly liked the horseback riding yesterday," Clarisa said.

"I remember Devin said you were raised in Wyoming, you learned to ride there?"

"I learned to ride when I was five. I was once married to a cowboy. He loved horses and we went riding frequently in those days."

"You're married?"

"He's dead now."

"Oh, I'm so sorry," Amelia said.

"That was a long time ago."

"He wasn't actually a cowboy?"

"Yes, well a rodeo cowboy, that's what he did for a living," Clarisa said looking out at the mountains in the distance.

"My goodness," Amelia said.

"Yeah, after he died, I decided to come to the big city. I came to San Francisco, took a course at the secretarial school, and I've been there ever since."

"Is there a man in your life now?" Amelia asked.

The question took Clarisa by surprise. After a second or two she said,"No, no one."

"Really…really?" Amelia responded.

What did that mean? Does she know or suspect something?

The caravan of jeeps pulled into the parking lot behind Ke'e beach. Everyone began piling out, carrying all his or her necessities for a day of fun in the sun. Aaron dashed down to the lagoon in front of the beach, threw down his towels and other gear and headed for the water. Beth began applying copious amounts of sun tan lotion to her still developing body. Amelia and Clarisa followed the Ashton men over to the shade of a tall stand of gnarled Kukui trees. Only six other employees had gathered in the circle around Billy Kamauu.

"OK, everyone here that's going on the hike?" Billy asked.

"Yeah, I guess that's all the hikers we have," Devin said.

"OK, just one rule, stay together, if we see you are falling behind we will try to stop and wait for you. Please catch up as quickly as possible. If you want to turn back, tell the people in front of you first. If I set too fast or too slow a pace, let me know. Any questions?" Billy asked.

None being offered, Billy set off down the trail followed by Devin and Carson. The other employees and Amelia and Clarisa brought up the rear. At first the trail gradually moved up the ridge and came to a point overlooking the Ke'e beach and the little lagoon. Amelia waved to Beth. Clarisa could see the large fish in the water of the lagoon. Out in the distance, the giant breakers were rolling in off an unimpeded run from the northern Pacific.

"I hope Aaron is not trying to be out in those," Amelia said.

"I see him down on the beach. He's ok," Clarisa said.

The trail went around a huge moss covered boulder and turned inward to the island for another assent. The whole party moved forward, Billy Kamauu setting a slow pace.

They turned a corner into a beautiful valley with a stream and a high towering waterfall coming down the side of the mountain. At one point, where the trail crossed the stream there was a small pool.

"Let's stop a minute," Amelia said.

"Sure," Clarisa said and they sat down, took off their tennis shoes and felt the water. It was extremely cold but it felt fine in the warm sunshine.

Amelia looked up the trail and could only barely see the last of the other members of the party, almost over the next portion of the trail that headed up and out of the valley. Clarisa began putting on her shoes. Is this the time for the next part of my plan? Do I have the guts to go to the next step? What if I get caught? Amelia finished tying her shoes. They jumped up and took off at a rapid rate.

"I guess we had better catch up," Amelia said.

"Sure."

The trail came out along a ledge. The trail was rather wide, but over on the seaward side was a steep drop down the cliff to the boiling sea below. Clarisa noticed a white puff of what looked like steam out in the ocean.

"Oh, Amelia, look, I think there are several whales spouting," Clarisa said pointing.

Amelia stopped and brought her hand up to shade her eyes as they both gazed out to sea looking for more evidence of the whales. Amelia squealed, "There, I see one, over to the left. Do you see it? I wonder if I can get a shot of that?" Amelia opened the leather carrying case strapped to her belt, which contained her camera.

Clarisa moved carefully over to the side of the trail and looked down. It was a least a thousand feet down to the black volcanic rocks. Only a narrow beach of sand stood between the rocks and the surge of the waves. Amelia moved over to see what Clarisa was looking at. Clarisa looked out to sea again.

"I see one out that way," she said.

Amelia pointed her camera out in the direction Clarisa had indicated. Clarisa took a step back and then over and behind Amelia. Clarisa looked up and down the trail. No one behind and the group had moved a good way over the next rise of the trail. Now! Seize the day! If you have the guts, if you don't want to be just a flunky all your life, do it. Do it now. Clarisa was about to put her hands on Amelia's back when she heard.

"Oh, hi, you two."

It was Betty Garrison coming from behind a large rock just up the trail. She had already thrown in the towel and was coming back down, giving up the hike.

"I think I have had enough, I'm heading back," Betty said between puffs of breath.

"I don't think I want to go much farther either," Amelia said.

"There is a beautiful viewpoint just over that ridge," Betty said. "You might want to see that before you go back. Well, I better get going while I can still move under my own power." Betty moved off, back toward the trailhead.

"Do you see the whale?" Amelia asked.

Clarisa turned and stared out to sea. God, that was close.

"No, let's head up, maybe you will have a better view ahead," Clarisa said.

They moved off again, up the trail, climbing even higher, back into the cliff side and out again toward the sea, always moving up. They came to the next lookout point. The view was spectacular, high green cliffs dropping sharply to the black lava formations, and waves breaking with white foam against the dark blue of the ocean. The drop was also superb. Clarisa thought it must be almost twelve hundred feet down that cliff.

"My goodness, we've had a pretty good climb," Amelia said trying to catch her breath.

"Let's see if we can see whales from here," Clarisa said. Again she moved over to the edge of the trail.

"Almost too high here to see them I would think," Amelia gasped as she came over to stand beside Clarisa. Amelia was gazing out at the ocean along with Clarisa.

"I think I see one out there," Clarisa said. Would she fall for it twice?

Amelia brought up her camera, scanning in the direction Clarisa had indicated. Clarisa took a step back. She looked carefully both up and down the trail. Nothing again. Her pulse was racing. She looked up the trail. No one. Now or never! She

pushed Amelia has hard as she could in the direction of the ocean. Amelia screamed

in surprise and tumbled down toward the edge of the trail. Desperately clawing at

the vegetation, she went over the cliff. Amelia screamed for what seemed an

eternity and then there was nothing. The sound of the surf below could barely be

heard. Clarisa had fallen to her knees toward the edge of the cliff. Trembling, she

pulled herself back.

"I had the guts to do it," she screamed aloud, her face to the sky. A sense of

relief filled her. Then she thought to herself, more calmly, "I made my kill. Of

course, this was not my first effort."

Two

The Beechcraft Bonanza banked to the left, entering the approach to the San Francisco International Airport. Frank Pullen was in the left seat, flying down a glide path as he had done so many times before, only at the controls of a Boeing 747. The sun reflected off the hills of Palo Alto, and you could see Stanford University. Matt Dawson was in the right seat keeping a close watch for other traffic in this one of the most congested of airways, at least in California. Through their headsets they could hear each other and the radio traffic.

"Matt, I have an idea," Frank said.

"Yeah?"

"Let's come up here for a New Year's party. This would be the place to greet the new century," Frank said.

"Could be fun. Can you believe that's only a few months from now," Matt said.

"But for now, let's take the Bay Tour," Frank said.

"What?" Matt answered.

"I've flown in here so many times, but I never got to circle the bay," Frank said.

"Bay Approach Control, this is Bonanza one three four gulf. I would like to go on the bay tour today. I'll take a clockwise bay tour, over Golden Gate, Sausalito and around back over Oakland. Also, could I have the vectors to SFO? Can you arrange?" Frank asked.

"Bonanza three four gulf, descend to two thousand five hundred. Be advised of a twin Cessna climbing out of twenty five for three thousand two miles at eleven o'clock," the controller responded.

"Thank you ma'am, going to twenty five hundred," Frank said.

Matt was also a pilot, an amateur compared to Frank, so he didn't look forward to flying in such a busy airspace.

Frank glanced over at his friend, "Relax, this is one of the most beautiful bays in the world."

"Sure."

Frank swung out to the west, over Highway 101, over Candlestick Park and downtown San Francisco. He went out over the Pacific and then north to follow the shoreline up and around to the Golden Gate Bridge. Matt watched three sailboats negotiate the bridge and beat up into the wind to the west, northwest.

"Some great sailing down there", Matt said. Matt Dawson was a private investigator, working out of San Diego where he lived on a sailboat docked at Harbor Island.

"You always have an eye out for the ragmen, don't you?" Frank said. Frank also had a boat at the same marina as Matt. Frank was a staunch motorboat man. He had a passion for the vintage diesel powered cabin cruisers.

The Bonanza banked to the right and moved over the northern part of the bay. Down below the bay was full of sight seeing boats, some ferrying people to and from the Rock, Alcatraz, the historic island prison, and smaller sailboats, trashing up and down in the brisk wind.

Matt was staring down into the bay when his saw something his brain couldn't explain, off slightly to the right and below them. It can't be a boat, the shape isn't right. It was becoming larger. It was another plane, coming directly at them.

"Frank, there is a plane directly off to our right and behind a hundred yards and coming up."

Frank didn't have any time to react as the other plane shot out in front of them, passing about fifty yards in front, and still climbing.

"That idiot..." Frank said.

"Bay Approach Control, this is Bonanza three four gulf. We have had a close call with a Cessna one eighty, climbing, past our position at two moving to eleven o'clock."

"Bonanza three four gulf, sorry. He never showed on our scope. He was VFR. Probably someone trying to scrud run without a transponder. Will try to contact him."

"Bay Approach Control, this is Bonanza three four gulf requesting vectors for SFO International," Frank said.

"OK, three four gulf, contact Tower Control on one twenty eight point six."

"Well, that was fun," said Frank as he brought the Bonanza into the airport landing approach. They were instructed to land on the right runway. As they touched the ground Matt watched a Boeing 777 land on the left runway. The large passenger plane touched down and sped on down the runway leaving them far behind.

"Always fun to land with the big boys," Matt said.

Frank just laughed.

Frank taxied up to the private plane terminal and cut the engine.

"You want to fuel it or bag it?" Frank asked.

They had rented the plane in San Diego for the flight to San Francisco. Matt and Frank had flown together many times. They alternated being in the right seat and the chore of seeing to the re-fueling of the plane for the return trip. The other would see to getting the bags into the terminal.

"You see to the fueling, I think they might see my hands still trembling from our little event," Matt said. He was kidding. Matt had faced many more dangerous situations during his brief career as a private detective.

"Yeah right. You warned me in time so that I was ready for that thing popping up in front of us," Frank said.

"What time are we meeting your friend?" Matt asked.

"At noon at the St. Francis bar," Frank said.

"When I get the bags in I'll go to the car rental desk," Matt said.

"OK."

Frank followed Matt out to the rental car parking lot, and he stopped beside a medium size white car and they put their luggage in the trunk.

"This is probably the only parking place available in San Francisco for this particular car," Matt said as he opened the front door.

"What are you trying to say?" Frank said, "I can always find a spot to park."

"Yeah, but you don't mind getting tickets," Matt said. Matt had arranged for a Ford Taurus. As Matt climbed in behind the wheel, it felt like being at the helm of a boat. He usually drove a Z3.

Matt steered a course for downtown San Francisco following the traffic choking one of the few freeways that had been rebuilt after the last earthquake. Getting off the freeway he found his way to Powell Street and on up to Union Square. He finally managed to get into the St. Francis parking garage. They found a spot to park and got out to head for the main lobby.

"Where did you know Mr. Justin?" Matt asked.

"Martin C. Justin is the Managing Director of the Children's Cancer Hospital in San Francisco. I met him when I was on the American Airlines Pilots' Association Board of Directors, in my other life," Frank said. "It was one of the charities we contributed to."

Frank was a retired American Airlines pilot who had to finish early because of an eyesight problem. Frank claimed to be the same age as Matt, forty, but Matt though he was a touch older, though Matt wasn't sure exactly by how much. Frank enjoyed a couple of inches of height over Matt and kept himself in good shape. He was too vain to wear glasses for anything but reading.

"This is about a problem he has with the hospital?" Matt asked.

"All I know is that he said he needed the services of a detective, one that was not connected locally to the San Francisco Police and that could get the job done," Frank said.

"I met Karl Mauldin once," Matt said.

"Doesn't count."

The elevator quickly delivered them to the main lobby of the Saint Francis.

"This old girl is elegant," Frank said.

"There's the bar," Matt said and they moved across to the entrance.

Frank studied the people at the table and bar for a moment.

"Frank, is that you?"

Matt and Frank turned and were greeted by Mr. Martin C. Justin. Justin was a distinguished looking middle aged man, graying temples, dark suit and subdued red tie.

"Frank, thank you so much for taking the time and trouble to come up. This must be your friend, Mr. Dawson?" Justin asked.

"Matt Dawson, pleased to meet you sir," Matt said.

"And I you, young man. Please, let's take that table over in the corner where we can talk," Justin said.

When they were seated, Justin said, "You two remind me of Indiana Jones and his partner."

Both Matt and Frank still had on their leather flying jackets.

"Sorry, we were late, so we didn't have time to change," Frank said.

"Not a problem. There's no dress code you're breaking here. Let's order some lunch," Justin said.

After the waitress had come and withstood Frank's interrogation as to the exact make up of the fish and chips, they all ordered.

"Now, Martin, what is the problem that you need Matt for?" Frank asked.

"Yes, well first, let me say that this is a delicate matter and I need your assurance that what you learn here will be kept confidential."

"Certainly," Matt said.

"Our hospital has been the beneficiary for years of the kind contributions of one of the leading industrialist in San Francisco, Mr. Devin Ashton. We have, in fact, come to rely on his continued generosity over the years to a point that I'm afraid, if changes are made in this financial support, we are in serious short term difficulties."

Matt looked at Frank with his "What the hell is he saying?" look.

"Why would this change?" Frank asked.

"Mr. Ashton has been the victim of a hit and run driver. He is now dead," Justin said.

"Was the hospital provided for in his will?" Matt asked.

"It was in the event of both Mr. and Mrs. Ashton passing. In that case the estate was to have been split between the hospital and the surviving children."

"You can't wait?" Matt asked.

"Well, that's not the problem, Mr. Ashton's wife, Clarisa, is said to be changing the will, leaving out not only Devin's children, save one, but also the hospital."

"What can you do about that?" Frank asked.

"We had a meeting with Carson Ashton. He's an attorney and Devin's oldest son. We believe that there may be grounds to file a lawsuit and have a judge put the assets into a trust."

"You think there may be some reason to think Mrs. Ashton had her husband killed?" Matt asked.

"That's what we need you to find out," Justin said.

"Are you the client or is Carson Ashton?" Matt asked.

"We think that the case might ultimately be stronger if the Hospital Board pays for your services," Justin said.

"How big is the Aston fortune?" Frank asked.

"It's estimated to be two hundred million," Justin said.

The food came and the interruption gave Matt a chance to think over the situation. His normal base of operations was San Diego. Could he be effective here in San Francisco? This wasn't the first job Matt had been offered through Frank's connections. He didn't want to let him down but Matt's basic operational mode was to bring his computer database query expertise to bear on a problem. How could this relate to a hit and run?

"Frank mentioned that you needed someone who was not connected to the San Francisco Police Department," Matt said.

"Yes, we think that would be better," Justin said.

"Why is that?" Matt asked.

"Had you heard of the Ashtons before I called Frank?" Justin asked.

"No, I'm afraid not," Matt said.

"Clarisa Ashton is a force in this town. She has been active in setting in motion the Ashton Arts Center over in Oakland, sponsoring relief programs for Native Americans and probably most importantly, being a big contributor to the local mayor's campaigns. You may have heard of his antics," Justin said.

"Oh yes, Willy Black, I have heard of his wild, even for San Francisco, parties," Frank said.

"Well, Clarisa is one of the beloved. The high profile, ultra liberal ones that politicians, the city ones in particular, curry favor with," Justin said. "We already have evidence that any suggestion of anything improper on her part will fall on deaf ears down at police headquarters."

"So what do you think, Matt?" Frank said.

"Well, wait, I appreciate your eagerness, but I have told Carson that we would talk with him before proceeding further," Justin said. "That is if you are interested, Mr. Dawson."

Frank looked over at Matt with his "Well?" face.

"Certainly, I might be able to help," Matt said.

"Splendid, I have a meeting set up with Carson and his sister, Beth, tomorrow at eleven. Here is the address," Justin said and he gave Matt one of his cards with an address written on the back. "You'll be there as well?" Justin asked Frank. Justin picked up the check.

"Yes, sure, thanks for lunch," Frank said as Justin rushed off.

"So what do you really think?" Frank asked.

"Let's see what the son says. Maybe I can better judge whether I could do anything or not."

"I'm sure you could help."

"Where did you get us reservations?" Matt asked.

"Comfort Inn by the Bay. It's only a few blocks from the wharf and you get really nice views of the bay."

"What do you want to do the rest of today?"

"Let's decide after we check in. I have a few calls to make," Frank said and they left the St. Francis and drove down toward Fisherman's Warf. They checked in and got two bay view rooms on the fifth floor.

Matt put his luggage in the corner of his room and pulled back the drapes from the windows across the end of the room. He picked up the phone and called Frank's room. "Boy, that's a great view. Have you stayed here before?" Matt asked.

"Yes, we stayed here occasionally when I was flying into San Francisco. How would you like to take a boat ride this afternoon?" Frank asked.

"What, the harbor cruise?"

"No, I just got off the phone with a pilot friend of mine. He lives in Dallas but flies into here on American. He keeps a sailboat here so that he can enjoy the bay. He says we can borrow it for the afternoon. Up to a little sailing?"

"You bet," Matt said. Near the top of Matt's list of favorite things to do in life was to sail.

In within the hour they had found the boat in the Marina Yacht Harbor. It was a Catalina 320, a thirty-foot sailboat.

"Can you run this rig?" Frank asked.

"Sure, it's a newer version of the one I used to keep here on the bay myself," Matt said. Matt had once lived in the area.

"Take the bow, Frank, and try to keep her straight as I back out. Don't forget to jump aboard," Matt said.

"You got it, Captain," Frank said.

Matt started the diesel and put the engine in reverse, at the slowest possible speed. The boat moved slowly out of the slip, Frank holding on and jumping aboard. Matt gently turned the boat into the space between the jungle of boat slips. He put the engine into forward and gently applied power. The Catalina moved steadily out in to San Francisco Bay. The brisk winds they had seen earlier had calmed though there was plenty left to power the sails. Frank took the helm and Matt raised the main and let out the jib. The wind was coming down the bay from the west, so Matt took the helm again and headed the boat out toward the northern end of the Golden Gate Bridge. The boat moved easily with a heel to starboard.

"I guess you got the hang of it," Frank said.

"Nothing like this bay, a fair wind and a good boat to sail," Matt said.

"This is a lot smaller than your boat."

Matt lived on his Sun Odyssey 45.2, about half again larger than the Catalina 320.

"It'll do, thanks so much, Frank, for setting this up. This is really great," Matt said.

Occasionally the wind would freshen and send spray over the bow. A few freighters were coming into the bay under the bridge. The scene reminded Matt of all the wonderful times he and Juliann had enjoyed on this bay. Matt had spent the earlier part of his life as a software developer and entrepreneur in Silicon Valley. He and his wife, Juliann had lived in Cupertino, south of San Francisco. She had loved to sail almost as much as Matt. He winced at the pain, like a sharp blow to the gut. It had been over three years now, but still the trauma of losing her hurt so much.

"What are you thinking about, Matt?" Frank asked.

Tears came into his eyes as he tried to keep his voice steady as he said, "Just thinking of all the times Juliann and I sailed here. We would take the bay tour as you called it. Sometimes go out to Angle Island, it took us about three hours to get up here from the South Bay."

"Those must have been good times," Frank said.

When Juliann died, Matt wanted out, to get away from the pain, so his partner Stan Morrison and some others bought out most of his shares of the software company they had built together. Matt moved down to San Diego to begin a second life.

The hours slipped by. They went under the Golden Gate, turned back and came back on a reverse tack, went out and around Alcatraz.

"Where do you want to eat, tonight?" Matt asked.

"Say, can you get us to Sausalito?"

"Sure, be there in under an hour."

"A good friend of mine has Italian restaurant there, might be fun to drop in on him."

"Is there anywhere you don't know someone, Frank?"

"Yeah, sure, anyplace American Airlines doesn't fly."

Matt headed the boat at the northern end of the Golden Gate again, to the little village of Sausalito. They tied up at a guest dock and walked the few blocks to Luigies.

After they had ordered and got their drinks Matt said,"I wonder what the law is, say if a wife is the beneficiary of a will and kills a husband. Does she still get the money?"

"Hmm, I don't know for sure. But as Justin said, I suppose some other interested party can get a judge to divert the money from the killer. If there is enough proof," Frank said.

"I wonder how much is enough? Remember, the jury let OJ off on the criminal charges, but another one found him guilty in the civil case," Matt said.

"In one case it's beyond reasonable doubt. In the other it's the preponderance of the evidence," Frank said.

"I don't know which this suit would be. We can ask Carson Ashton tomorrow. I'm looking forward to getting a new case to work on," Matt said.

Luigi came over and huged Frank, "Long time since you were here, Frank."

Their dinners came.

"Enjoy, enjoy," Luigi said.

After a fine pasta dinner, and a couple of drinks with Luigi, they sailed back across the Bay to the marina, catching the sunset.

Three

Matt and Frank had an early walk down to the wharf area. They got some

breakfast at a small place near the Maritime Museum. The little restaurant catered to

the local fishermen. Matt and Frank couldn't help overhearing the captains swapping

info on where they found a catch or ran into trouble.

"Not just us tourists in here," Frank said.

"Some of these guys talk a good game. I wonder if they actually catch anything

or just spend their time entertaining each other," Matt said.

After breakfast they returned to the hotel and got ready for the meeting

downtown. They were both sporting suits and ties as they got on the elevator of the

high rise building in which Carson Aston had his law office. The receptionist ushered

them into the conference room. They were the last to arrive. Sitting around the

table were Carson Ashton, Beth, his sister, and Martin C. Justin. Carson and Martin

got up and Martin introduced Frank and Matt.

Carson Ashton was a tall and fit man, with blond hair and an air about him that

said top-drawer lawyer. He returned to his seat after shaking Frank and Matt's hands

and said, "Gentlemen this is my sister, Beth Agasture. Well, we can get started now.

Martin here has given me some of your background Mr. Dawson, I wonder if you

would mind answering a few questions?"

"Sure, that would be fine," Matt said.

"First, as I think Martin has mentioned to you, I would have normally used one of

my local people for this investigation but as every one of them has ties to the police

department we decided it would be wise to find someone else. How long have you

been doing this work, Mr. Dawson?"

"A little over three years, though I did work for my father in Denver, who is also

an attorney for several years during college," Matt said.

"And are you a member of NALI?" Carson asked.

"Yes, I have been a member for two years," Matt said.

"What's that?" Frank asked Matt.

"The National Association of Legal Investigators," Matt said.

"Frank tells me that Matt has helped out on several delicate situations that he is aware of," Martin said.

"You were on the American Airline Pilot's Board I understand?" Carson asked Frank.

"Yes, I had to retire early, but that's where I met Martin, we think his hospital is doing a badly needed job," Frank said.

"Yes, my father was a strong supporter also, in fact as Martin may have told you the hospital was to received the largest share of the estate," Carson said.

"So, Mr. Dawson, what did you do prior to becoming a detective?" Carson asked.

"I think of my self as a computer specialist who uses that tool to aid in investigations. My partner and I started a company, Softbase, which specialized in prospective employee profiles. When I sold out, and even today, the company is the leader in that market," Matt said.

"I think I have heard of that company, my father was a venture capitalist you know, he may have had a position in your company," Carson said.

"It's possible, I sold out a few years ago, my partner handled the financing, I ran the technical part of the company," Matt said.

"Beth, do you have any questions?" Carson said.

Beth sat on Carson's right, in a fashionable beige suit, smoking with her arms crossed. She was a sun bleached blond with her hair tied back in a ponytail. The sun had not been kind to her complexion. She was deeply tanned and looked older than her thirty something years.

"No, I'm sick of thinking that this vile creature Clarisa is going to take all of our money. Let's get on with it," Beth said.

"Right, as you may have concluded, we think there could be something more to our father's death than an accidental hit and run," Carson said.

"What have the police concluded?" Matt asked.

"They think that he was killed by accident, he was going to his car at his tennis club. There is not much lighting in the area. He had his trunk open and was putting in his tennis bag when the car struck him. There was one witness. The car sped off into the night," Carson said.

"What does the witness say?" Matt asked.

"He gave only a vague description of the car. The police say that it was probably someone who belonged to the club as you can only get access to the club from a long driveway that goes out to the main street. There wouldn't be any drive by traffic," Carson said.

"That's if it was an accident," Frank said.

"Exactly," Carson said.

"What is it that you need?" Matt asked.

"Right now, we need enough information to convince a judge that there may have been foul play involving Clarisa, my father's second wife, so that he will put the Aston estate in a trust until we can litigate the matter," Carson said.

"Why do you suspect her?" Matt asked.

"I think a little history is needed to answer that. My father was a successful venture capitalist. I think he always thought that his wise judgements of people in business carried over into his personal life. He and my mother were married almost twenty years. She was from a prominent old San Francisco family. She died in an accident in Hawaii in nineteen seventy-eight. I was in law school. We were all shocked and saddened by her loss, but my father suffered the worst. Just two years later, he married his secretary, Clarisa. I didn't know what to do when I heard about this, I knew Clarisa and my father had been close, but I never thought he would think of marrying her."

"That's when we got the other detective," Beth said.

"Exactly, under the advice of my father's attorney, but not with my father's knowledge, we hired an investigator to look into Clarisa's past."

"What did he find?" Matt asked.

"I have a copy of his report here," and Carson shoved a stack of papers across the desk. "The main point he found was that Clarisa had a lover a few years earlier, another wealthy man. We think Clarisa was expecting to be wed, but the man had other ideas. He was found dead in his tub, an accidental drowning due to an overdose of drugs and alcohol, they said."

"Seems like I have heard the word accident at lot," Frank said.

"You can add another to the list, Clarisa comes from Wyoming. At one point she was married to a cowboy, a rodeo cowboy. He died in an accident during one of his rides," Carson said.

"Has anyone ever accused Clarisa of a crime?" Matt asked.

"Never," Carson said.

"Did you show your father the report?" Matt asked.

"I tried to, but he wouldn't have any of it. As I said, he thought his judgement about people was infallible," Carson said.

"Do you have any other brothers or sisters?" Matt asked.

"Just Aaron," Beth said.

"Aaron is on a different wave length when it comes to Clarisa," Carson said.

"They both are trash," Beth said.

"Aaron is a dreamer, always wanting to do something big, as long as it doesn't involve any real effort," Carson said.

"He and Clarisa are thick as thieves," Beth said.

"Do you live here in San Francisco?" Matt asked Beth.

"No, I'm married to the tennis pro at Los Gatos Tennis Ranch in Santa Barbara. We live there, on the resort. You may have heard of my husband, Peter Agasture. He was ranked fourteenth a few years ago." Beth said.

"Sorry, no," Matt said.

"In all my experience there are rarely that many accidents in anyone's life," Carson said.

"I think you can see why we are suspicious," Martin said.

"We think there may be a pattern here, but we need enough proof to show to the judge. Can you get us that proof, Mr. Dawson?" Carson asked.

"It seems like you have plenty to investigate, and a lot of time has passed. But yes, it's possible I may be able to find what you need," Matt said.

"We need a guarantee," Beth said.

"That would be difficult for Mr. Dawson to give," Martin said.

"All I can guarantee you is that I will give this my best efforts," Matt said.

"Yes, well, I think that's all we can expect," Carson said.

"As Mr. Justin has explained you will actually be paid by the Hospital Board. But Martin and I have agreed that you will be working under my direction. Do you have any questions?" Carson said.

"One, how are your relations with Mrs. Ashton?" Matt asked.

"Cool and correct. At this point I don't think she knows that we feel she might be involved," Carson said.

"Could you call her and tell her that you asking me to find the person that was driving the hit and run car and that I will be coming by to see her?" Matt asked.

"Yes, I think she will want to appear to be cooperating," Carson said.

"Also, if you could give me the name of the lead police detective on the case," Matt said.

"I will, but I don't think you will have much help there," Carson said.

"Alright, I'll do the best I can," Matt said and all but Beth stood up and moved to the door.

"Here's my card with my direct line number and that detective's name," Carson said.

"I'll keep you informed at least every few days," Matt said.

"When is the will to be probated?" Martin asked Carson.

"The beginning of the month. We need something before then if possible," Carson said.

"Not a lot of time," Frank said.

The next morning Frank and Matt sat at a small table, on the second floor deck at Ghirardelli Square, with a fine view of the Bay.

"I'm not sure this looks like I'm giving my best effort," Matt said.

"We're reviewing the other detectives notes aren't we. Why shouldn't we do it in a beautiful place," said Frank.

"Right," Matt said as he finished reading the next page of the notes and passed the page over to Frank.

"You want another cup of chocolate?" Frank said.

"No thanks."

The other detective's name was Glen Easton. The report detailed his actions after Carson had hired him. He found out where Clarisa lived and followed her for a few days, finding the places she ate and what she did in her time off from work. At that time she was Devin Aston's personnel secretary and she spent a lot of time in his company. Easton was an ex San Francisco cop and somehow he managed to find a police report about a previous boy friend a few years before she started working at Ashton Ventures. Howard Peterson was a successful stockbroker, listed as one of the most eligible bachelors in San Francisco at the time. Clarisa's statement was that she had been with him on the afternoon that he died but she had left early in the evening, wanting to be ready for an interview the next day. The lab work on Peterson indicated that he had a high blood alcohol level and a trace of drugs in his system. He died of drowning. The detective on the case was suspicious of Clarisa but there was no evidence that she caused the death. The death was ruled accidental.

Easton found a person who had known Clarisa in her previous job. He got the impression from this ex-friend that Peterson had promised to marry Clarisa, but then had told her that he changed his mind. Clarisa was reportedly furious.

Easton found out that Clarisa was born in 1942 in Cheyenne, Wyoming. Her maiden name was Clarisa Wilkes, the daughter of a curio shop owner, Harley Wilkes. Somehow, Easton had managed to get a medical report on Clarisa and found out that she had had an abortion. The report did not detail when this had occurred, but it did note that Clarisa could not have any more children.

The report concluded with the information that Clarisa had married a man named Dudley Haynes in 1960. Dudley was a none-too-successful professional rodeo rider. He died in 1966 in a rodeo accident. No details of the accident were available.

Shortly after Dudley died Clarisa came to San Francisco and waited tables until she had enough money to go to the Barriston Secretarial School. She had several secretarial positions before going to work for Ashton Ventures.

Easton was suspicious of the death of the first Mrs. Ashton. This was a hiking accident that occurred in 1978 in Hawaii. He was able to find a witness that was on the same hike as Amelia Ashton, Mrs. Betty Garrison. She had seen Mrs. Ashton on the trail shortly before her accident. She refused to say anything useful. Easton thinks she was afraid for her job as she was still working for Ashton Ventures at the time he talked to her.

"Clarisa has had an interesting life," Frank said as he laid down the last page of the report.

"People around her do seem to be accident prone," Matt said.

"So, what's your first move?" Frank said.

"Not what's our first move?" Matt said.

"No Matt, sorry but I need to get back. Laura is having this shindig that she's been planning for a few months. I promised I'd be there." Frank was Matt's unofficial helper. Matt had talked to him about becoming a partner, but he wanted to be free to go when and where he liked, such as now to keep his friend Laura happy. Laura Jacobs was an ex Navy nurse who was the widow of a naval officer. She was a year or two younger than Frank and in trim condition. She and Frank played several games of doubles each week with their tennis buddies. Laura and her husband had their home on Coronado. Frank and her husband had been good friends. Matt thought she was an attractive lady and he really liked her. She was always the life of the party.

"OK, I understand. You fly the Bonanza back and I'll take commercial," Matt said.

"Worried about taking off from SFI?" Frank said.

"No, it costs too much to have that thing sitting on the ground."

"What's your first step?" Frank asked.

"I think I'll look up the police detective assigned to the hit and run," Matt said.

"Sounds like a place to start. Professional courtesy as well."

"Let's walk down the wharf and have one last fish dinner together before you go back," Matt said.

"Sounds like a plan."

Four

Matt walked up to the desk at the San Francisco Police Department's main station and asked for Detective Gaylord Kerns.

"What do you want to see Detective Kerns about?" the desk Sargent asked.

"I'm a private investigator working on a hit and run case he is handling," Matt said.

The Sargent picked up a phone and dialed Kerns's extension and relayed Matt's request.

"Head up those stairs. It's the second office on your left."

Matt headed up the stairs. The building was old but well maintained. Numerous police officers were coming and going on the stairway. The second office on the left was labeled "Homicide". Matt stopped at the desk inside the door and came up to the clerk.

"Kerns?" Matt asked.

"Third desk on the middle isle," the clerk responded.

The office was laid out with three rows of desks, each with one side chair and a filing cabinet.

Matt came up to the one with Kerns's nameplate. Kerns was on the phone.

"Now Arthur you are my significant other but I've told you many times I do not like him, he just isn't a nice person. If you want to see him away from our home, fine, but I have my rights. Please respect them," Kerns said. He glanced up and saw Matt sitting at his side chair. "I have to go now." He slammed down the receiver.

"Yes, what can I do for you?"

"My name is Matt Dawson. I have been hired to look into the death of Mr. Devin Ashton. I think you are handling the case?"

"You're not the insurance investigator are you? They said Global World had assigned an investigator into this case," Kerns asked.

"No. Why would they do that?"

"It is strange. Apparently a clause in Mr. Ashton's policy that said it wouldn't pay off if the death was murder."

"I've never heard of that one," Matt said.

Matt handed Kerns his card.

"Yes, Mr. Ashton's death was a terrible thing, let me get the file," Kerns said and he turned around and fumbled through the file cabinet. He brought out a thick folder and scanned through the first few pages.

"At the moment, it looks like it was an accident so I was about to send it to another unit. We only investigate murder here," Kerns said.

"I wonder if I could get a copy of your report?" Matt asked.

"Well, it's not done as yet, but, let's see, if you don't mind my preliminary version. Bobby," Kerns called over to an assistant. "Shoot me a copy of these pages," Kerns said and Bobby came over and got the pages.

"Could you tell me what you know?" Matt asked.

"I suppose so, Mr.Ashton was at his tennis club, just leaving, putting his things in the trunk of his car. Have you been out to the club?"

"No, not yet."

"Well, it's a relatively small parking lot. There are only a few hundred members of the club, a rectangle, with Ashton's car up near the entrance to the club. The hit and run car came around the corner and hit him, knocked him forward and ran right over him. Crushed his skull."

"The driver must have been going fast, for a parking lot."

"Yes, probably drunk or something, there was another member further down that was getting into his car. He heard the collision and saw the car drive past him go up to the exit, slam on the brakes and spin out down the lane to the main street," Kerns said.

"How much help was the witness in identifying the car?"

"Very little, all he can say is that it was a late model General Motors sedan and that it was a dull color, there isn't much lighting in that parking lot."

"He didn't see the driver?"

"Apparently not, he said he was concerned with the victim at that point."

"Have you turned up anything else?" Matt asked.

"We have the list of members of the club, there are three hundred and sixty I think, and we are checking out the types of cars they drive. This dull late model fits almost everyone's car so we are mainly relying on the flyer we are sending out to all the body repair shops. That will usually pinpoint someone in a hit and run, eventually," Kerns said.

"Could I get a copy of that list?" Matt asked.

"Sure, here you go," Kerns said as he handed Matt the membership list.

"Have you talked to Mrs. Ashton?"

"Poor woman, yes, I was the one that had to tell her about her loss."

"Did you go over to her home that night?"

"Yes, the Astons live over in Pacific Heights, beautiful place, she was devastated."

"This accident made her a wealthy woman," Matt said.

"What are you saying? She was a wealthy woman already. Being from out of town, perhaps you don't know all the things that this woman has done for San Francisco."

"Sorry, I guess I don't," Matt said.

"Well, Clarisa Ashton is one of the city's most prominent citizens. She is behind many of the better aspects of the San Francisco lifestyle. The Ashton Regional Center for the Arts is the envy of many of the people in the art world. She has been quite supportive of the Gay community, and her position on gun control has been warmly received."

"You're quite a fan of hers," Matt said.

"I suppose I am but if there were reason to believe she was involved I certainly would follow up on that," Kerns said.

"Did you ask her where she was that evening?" Matt asked.

"Of course, she said she was at home, and her maid backed her up on that," Kerns said.

"Detective, I want to thank you for your help," Matt said.

"Mr. Carson Ashton called me and said you would be coming by, so I want to be as helpful to the family as I can be. I would expect you to return the favor, and let me know of anything that you turn up," Kerns said.

"Yes, I will Detective, thanks again." Matt took the few pages of the report and the membership list and left the way he had come.

The next morning after a walk along the bay, Matt busied himself in his hotel room setting up his portable computer in a choice spot so that he could look out at the Bay at any time he was not looking at the screen. It was time to do the grunt work on the people in this case. He started his Personnel Profiler program.

Matt had first developed the Profiler as a product to be sold to HRs, Human Resource Departments, to do automated background checks of prospective employees. Stan Morrison, his partner, had been a marvel in finding ways to get in to see the HR people in some of the biggest companies. The Profiler was far and away the best seller of its type of product. Matt had extended the Profiler to meets the needs of his "Cybernetic Personnel Research and Investigations." The Profiler connected to the Internet and could start the direct access of multiple databases on the web with whatever small amount of information the user had on a particular person, such as name or social security number. Matt used a technique that bypassed the normal pretty screens the casual Internet user sees and went directly to the target databases. These query requests went out to several hundred sites and the access to these databases went on simultaneously. The genius of the program was that it mapped back the responses from all these different databases into a single coherent report. A person who had not changed their name or social security number and had lived in several states might have several hundred hits.

Matt fed in the names, Devin Ashton, Amelia Ashton, Clarisa Ashton, Martin C. Justin, Beth Ashton Agasture, Aaron Ashton, Betty Garrison and Glen Easton, the original detective investigating Clarisa. For good measure, Matt included San Francisco Detective Gaylord Kerns and Howard Peterson, Clarisa's friend that drowned while in his bathtub. Matt scanned down Detective Kerns's report and found the witness to the hit and run, Karl Zoltang. He added Zoltang to the list. Within half an hour a large output print file had collected on Matt's computer. When the processing was complete, Matt transferred the output print file to a floppy disk and went down to the lobby and out on the street.

He found a print shop a few blocks down Lombard Street. He gave the floppy to the clerk and after a few minutes he had two inches of print out. He picked up a coffee and a bagel and headed back to his room to study the reports that the Profiler program had produced.

He sorted through the stack of paper and found what the system had found out about Clarisa. Clarisa had received numerous awards in the last ten years, such as humanitarian of the year for several different groups. She had been selected for numerous charity boards and was the Chairwoman of the board of the Aston Regional Center for the Arts. She was a member of the Lake Merced Country Club, and a winner in a "Women in Full Life Golf Tournament". The system found that she had been born Clarisa Wilkes in Cheyenne, Wyoming plus the added little item, that she had a brother. David Wilkes was still living in Cheyenne. She was a member of the Democratic Party and on a Fund Raising Committee for that organization. All in all she was a busy lady, Matt thought.

He found no criminal references, not even a parking ticket.

The Profiler scanned several major newspaper story files, spanning issues over the last five years, and numerous references were found to articles concerning or at least mentioning Clarisa Ashton. One even mentioned Clarisa's meeting with Mother Teresa.

Matt arranged the other reports on the other names he had fed the program, none were as thick as Clarisa's.

Matt looked through Aaron Ashton's file next. Matt noted that it revealed that Aaron only finished a year and a half of college. Had never been married, had been the President of several corporations, Bayside Entertainment, Roaring Room Incorporated and Roaring Forties Girl, Inc.

All were now out of business. There was also a bankruptcy only two years ago. More puzzling, Aaron had a Porsche 914 registered in his name.

Matt stretched and got up and walked around the room. It was time to talk to some of these people. He picked up the phone and asked Carson Ashton to get an appointment for him with Clarisa. Might as well go to the source. Carson called back, Clarisa would be glad to talk to him at ten this morning. Carson gave Matt the address. Matt had to scramble to be presentable to the heiress.

It was straight up ten o'clock when Matt pulled up to the address on Broadway in the Pacific Heights area of San Francisco. The homes were old and all carefully reconditioned. Matt drove though the gate and up the short driveway, past the English garden. A red Porsche 914 was sitting on the circle drive in front of the house, so Matt parked his Ford behind it. The house had three floors and a three-car garage off on the left side as you faced the entryway. Two doors of the garage were open, revealing a Lexus RX 400 sport utility. The other open space was empty. Matt noticed another small car, probably a sports car, parked under a tree out in front of the garage, covered.

"Lots of rolling stock," Matt thought to himself.

Matt went to the door and pushed the button. The door chime sounded like it was break time on NBC. After a few minutes, a maid opened the door. She was young, Latin and dazzlingly pretty.

"Yes," she said.

"I have an appointment with Mrs. Ashton. Matt Dawson is my name."

"OK, please come in."

Matt entered through the huge door. The main entry hall was impressive. The large stairway to the left went up and around to the next two floors. Three floors up, a stained glass in the ceiling over the entryway bathed the room in a greenish, bluish light almost giving the impression of being in another world. One of the two doors on the left evidently went down a hall to the garage. To the right, double doors were open to the living room. Matt noticed a small elevator off the hall to the right.

"Wait in here, please," the young lady said and indicated the living room.

Matt entered the room. He was not an art collector, but he was impressed. The room was filled with Western Art, statues of horses, cowboys, buffaloes, and Indians. One picture on the wall seemed somewhat familiar. It must be a copy of a Remington, he thought. He went over to the painting. It was not a copy and it was an authentic Remington.

The maid returned and said, "Mrs. Ashton would like you to join her at the pool, please."

Matt followed her back into the entry hall and down and out toward the rear of the home, outside to a patio beside a small pool.

Clarisa Ashton was seated at a small poolside table, holding her eyeglasses, which were secured by a gold chain around her neck. Matt was stunned. He knew she was fifty-six, but it seemed like he was looking at a much younger Julie Andrews, stepping right out of her role from the Sound of Music. She smiled, extended her hand and said, "Good morning, I'm Clarisa and you must be the detective Carson has

hired."

"Yes Ma'am, Matt Dawson," he said. He took her hand. He didn't know if she wanted

to shake or if he was supposed to kiss it.

He decided on a gentle shake.

"Thank you for seeing me on such short notice," Matt said.

"Yes, would you like some coffee?"

"Thank you, yes," Matt said.

Clarisa poured Matt some coffee from a silver server and he sat down across from

her.

"I'm sorry for your loss," Matt said.

"Oh, yes. Devin was such a dear. He gave me everything I needed."

"I have a few questions," Matt said.

A door off the right of the back of the house opened. A young man in his mid

thirties came out in a robe. He had dark, slicked back hair and didn't seem to be in

a good mood. He didn't even look over in the direction of the small table that Matt

and Clarisa were sitting, but went down a path straight to the far end of the pool.

Matt watched him, expecting him to come over to the table, but he went up to the

small diving board, dropped his robe, hopped up on the board and jumped in, all

without the benefit of a bathing suit.

Matt sipped his coffee and watched the swimmer breaststroke down the pool and

turn and do an Australian crawl back to the diving board. He pulled himself out of the

water, picked up his robe and retraced his steps back to the house and over to the

door Matt had come out of. Never once, did he glance over Matt's way.

"Aaron has his little morning ritual," Clarisa said.

Matt thought, "His little mid-morning ritual."

"That was Aaron Ashton, Carson's brother?" Matt asked.

"Yes, sometimes he can be a bore, perhaps he will join us shortly," Clarisa said.

"He lives here, then?" Matt asked.

"Yes, he has always found it easier. Devin always thought his mother spoiled him too much. I think he has never been able to reach his full potential. He has some marvelous business ideas," Clarisa said.

"He has started several ventures?" Matt asked.

"He has been trying to get a new type of entertainment going here in San Francisco. He is bringing back some of the class that the supper clubs had in the thirties."

"Mrs. Ashton, I wanted to ask you about the night your husband was killed. He was at the tennis club I understand?" Matt said.

"He played tennis regularly on Wednesdays. He was getting in his car they tell me, when someone, possibly some other club member, struck him down. Hit and run is so awful," Clarisa said and she reached into her pocket for a small handkerchief.

"Do you know anyone at his tennis club that might have a reason for murdering him?"

"Murder? I thought it was just a horrible accident. Still, I suppose it's possible. Several of the members are also people who have interests in various investments that Devin's company had backed. Sometimes, Devin would invest in a company, and if it was clear to him, at least, that it wasn't going to work out, he would have to pull out. Sometimes pulling back some of the funds these people thought were committed. Sometimes, it would cause hard feelings. But, in business, you must look after your own stockholders first," Clarisa said.

"Could you name anyone specific who would fit that description?" Matt asked.

Before she could answer, the cell phone sitting on the table rang. Clarisa picked it up.

"Yes, Elaine, how are you," Clarisa said and she reached for the coffeepot.

Clarisa covered the mouthpiece and shouted back to the house, "Maria, Maria."

There was no response.

"I must be stupid to keep that girl on. Could you be a dear and have Maria get us a fresh pot?" Clarisa said to Matt.

"Sure."

Matt picked up the coffee server and walked back to the house, opened the door into the hall. He noticed droplets of water, heading down the hall toward the front of the house and off to the left. Matt went through the opening to his left, which led to the kitchen. Maria was busy polishing the small dining table at the end of the area. "Mrs. Ashton would like a fresh pot," Matt said as Maria looked up.

Matt thought he heard Maria say something under her breath.

"I'll have to make a fresh pot," she said.

Matt watched as she filled a small grinder with coffee beans, and ran the grinder for half a minute or so.

Aaron came into the kitchen, dressed this time in a fancy sport shirt and khakis. He went up to the coffeepot, reached up to the cabinet and pulled out a coffee cup.

"I'm just making fresh," Maria said.

Matt extended his hand and said, "Hello, I'm Matt Dawson."

He wasn't sure Aaron was going to shake his hand, but at last he did and said, "Why are you here this morning? Looking for a donation to yet another good cause?"

"No, your brother hired me to see if we can find the person that killed your father," Matt said.

Aaron glanced up, startled, and said, "Oh."

"Maria, I understand you were here the evening Mr. Ashton was killed?"

Maria and Aaron shared a quick glance. "Yes," Maria said.

"What were you doing that evening?" Matt asked.

"I was in my room, watching television," Maria said.

"Mr. Ashton, were you here as well?" Matt asked.

"In the house? Yes, I was," Aaron said.

"What were you doing that evening?"

"I was reading a book," Aaron said.

"Maria, was Mrs. Ashton here that night also?" Matt asked.

"Yes, sir."

"Where is your room, Maria?" Matt asked.

"Back over on that side of the house," Maria said. She indicated the side opposite to the garage.

"Is your bedroom over on that side as well?" Matt asked Aaron.

"No, it's over the garage."

"And where was Mrs. Ashton?" Matt asked Maria.

"In her bedroom on the third floor I suppose, though she might have been in the Jacuzzi on the top deck."

"Did you speak to your step mother that evening Mr. Ashton?" Matt asked.

"No, just read my book," Ashton said.

Matt was tempted to ask the title of his book, but he thought that would be pushing it. He didn't think Aaron looked to be the book reading type.

"Mrs. Ashton mentioned your father might have had enemies at his tennis club, do you know anyone like that Mr. Ashton?"

"No, he stopped talking to me about business matters a long time ago," Aaron said.

The coffee was ready and Maria filled the silver server.

"I'll bring it out," Maria said.

"Thanks for you your help," Matt said.

"Sure, I want to find the killer too," Aaron said.

Matt rejoined Clarisa on the patio. She was still on the phone.   Maria left the coffee and Matt poured himself a fresh cup.

As Clarisa continued to talk to the person on the other end about details of the upcoming benefit, Matt studied Clarisa's face. It was tight, yes. She had had several face lifts, though it wasn't too noticeable. She finally hung up the phone.

"Sorry, these things take so much planning."

"Just a few questions, you were about to tell me if you could think of the name of any person at the tennis club that might have a grudge against your husband," Matt said.

"Devin never got into details about his business dealings. He wanted to get away from the pressure when he was with me," Clarisa said.

"You were here the evening he was killed. I think the police told me the accident happened around nine?" Matt asked.

"Yes, I had a guest list to go over, watched one show on TV I think and spent some time in the Jacuzzi. I had been in bed a while when Maria came up and knocked on the door and told me the police were downstairs," Clarisa said.

"When did they get here?" Matt asked.

"It must have been after eleven," Clarisa said. "That nice detective Kerns is the one that gave me the news, he was so considerate."

"He's a big fan of yours too," Matt thought.

"Did you go over to the scene or to the hospital?" Matt asked.

"No, I called Carson and he came over, the police said it would be of no use to go over to the tennis club as they had already taken Devin's body away," Clarisa said. "Carson was close to his father, he was very upset."

"And Aaron was at home as well?"

"Yes."

"The maid Maria also?"

"I don't see why it's important, but, yes she was in her room," Clarisa said.

"Did you speak to her after you had gone to your bedroom?" Matt asked.

Clarisa glared slightly at Matt. "I often call down to her to bring me up another bottle of wine, but I don't remember if I did that on the evening I lost Devin," Clarisa said.

"Thanks Mrs. Ashton, I may want to ask you about a few other things, but that's all the questions I have for now," Matt said.

He got up shook her hand again, and met Maria at the door back into the house. Maria walked Matt out to the front door.

"Is that your car under the tree?" Matt asked.

"Yes, it's a Miata," Maria said.

"Nice car," Matt said as he went through the door.

"Thanks."

"Goodbye."

Five

Matt headed back down Broadway. Battling the one way streets, he found a group of Chinese restaurants on Grant and miraculously, a parking spot. Taking in his brief case he took a table at the rear of the room. After ordering, he opened his case and took out his Profiler Reports. What had he learned from his visit with Clarisa? He understood now why almost everyone was unable to think of her doing a criminal act. Would Julie Andrews do murder? He got an idea about the nature of Aaron Ashton and had met the maid, Maria. Was there a problem between Clarisa and Maria? Was there something else between Maria and Aaron? Clarisa seemed to believe that someone at the tennis club had it in for Devin Aston. Could that be true? Matt sorted down through the Profiler Report to find the section on the witness to the hit and run. Karl Zoltang was the president of Zoltang and Associates, Insurance Agency. Matt took out his cell phone and placed a call to Mr. Zoltang.

The receptionist answered on the first ring. "Zoltang and Associates, how may I help you?"

"Mr. Karl Zoltang, please, this is Matt Dawson calling."

"May I tell him what this is regarding?"

"Yes, it's about the death of Devin Aston," Matt said.

After a few minutes of elevator music Zoltang came on the line.

"This is Karl Zoltang, how may I help you?"

"Mr. Zoltang, I'm a private investigator, hired by Carson Ashton to look into his father's death. I understand you were the only witness."

"Yes, it was so tragic and upsetting, I didn't know Mr. Ashton well, but it was shocking to see him killed that way," Zoltang said.

"Yes sir, I wonder if you could spare me a few minutes to go over what you saw?"

"Certainly, do you know where my office is?"

"I was hoping we could meet at the tennis club and you could go over exactly what you saw, where you planning to go there anytime soon?"

"Why yes, I have a court for this evening. How long will this take?"

"I would think no more than half an hour."

"Alright, why don't we meet at the club bar at say five this evening?"

"Yes, that would be fine, I'll see you at five, I suppose I'll be the one not in a tennis outfit," Matt said.

"It's a small place, I'm sure we'll make contact, see you there." Zoltang hung up.

Matt's lunch came and he put away his papers. The Chinese food was excellent. After lunch he headed generally back toward his hotel. He saw a large bookstore on the next corner. He pulled around back and parked. He went inside and found the section on cars. Scanning down the rack of every conceivable kind of book about cars, he came to what he was looking for, a current listing of used automobiles, complete with several pictures of each model of car.

Returning to his hotel room, Matt decided to call Frank and see how Laura's party had turned out.

"How did the party go?" Matt asked when Frank came on the line.

"Fine, everyone showed up and we had a nice meal prepared at the club, Laura really enjoys seeing all her old friends."

"Did Quincy come?"

"Yes, she wasn't happy that you didn't make it back," Frank said.

"Yeah, I told her I thought I would be able to but this is going to take some time," Matt said.

"Have you met the heiress?"

"Yes, she is quite impressive, the last person you would be suspicious of," Matt said.

"What's the next move?"

"I need to talk to Carson Ashton again and I have an appointment with the hit and run eye witness this evening," Matt said.

"Do you want me to come up and kibitz?" Frank asked.

"Let me get a day or two more into this and then I might need your help," Matt said.

"OK, have you called Qunicy?" Frank asked.

"Not yet."

"Probably be the thing to do," Frank said.

"Right, talk to you later," Matt said and hung up the phone. Matt dialed Quincy's work number. Matt and Quincy had been dating for a few months. Quincy Ferris was one of the evening news anchors at Channel Three in San Diego. She was a well-known personality, having been at the TV station for several years. Many people recognized her when she was out with Matt made him uncomfortable.

"Ms. Ferris office," the secretary said.

"Hi, this is Matt, could I talk to Quincy," Matt said.

"Sure, just a second."

"I thought you were coming back for Laura's party," Quincy said.

"I had hoped to, but this case is going to take a while," Matt said.

"When are you coming back?"

"Don't know yet."

After a pause, "Frank says you both went sailing," Quincy said.

"Yes, it was great, we did that after our first meeting with the clients, Frank has connections everywhere it seems," Matt said.

"Well, are you lonesome, at least?"

"Certainly, if this drags out a while, do you want to come up for the weekend?"

"I've got some promotion stuff to do this weekend, but let's see how it works out, might be fun," Quincy said.

"OK, I do miss seeing you," Matt said.

"I guess I'll have to settle for that for now."

"I'll call you again, in a couple of days," Matt said and hung up.

Next, he called Carson Ashton. After Matt got by his secretary, Carson answered.

"Mr. Dawson, how did the meeting go with Clarisa?"

"She was cooperative. She has a theory that there are people in your father's tennis club who might have had ill feelings toward him because of his various financial transactions," Matt said.

"When you are dealing the type of high stake propositions my father handled every day, yes there could be people who get hurt financially, and there are probably some of them that belong to that club."

"Are there any that you know of specifically?" Matt asked.

"On one start up my father had to pull back the initial financing on Carter-Hillman Net-Centric, an Internet dream that was just that. I think Philip Hillman may be a member of the Tanurack Club."

"Have they made any threats that you know of?" Matt asked.

"Only to sue, which they did. That is one of the cases I'm handling, but Mr. Dawson, we are more interested in what part Clarisa might have played in my father's death."

"Yes sir, I understand, but if you are to convince a judge that an impartial investigation was made, some of these allegations should be noted," Matt said.

"Yes, you're correct about that."

"The maid and your brother Aaron say that Clarisa was at home when your father was killed," Matt said.

"She may have employed some one else to do this," Carson said.

"Is there any problem between the maid, Maria, and your step mother, that you know of?" Matt asked.

"Yes, there is. I am surprised that Clarisa still keeps Maria around. Her name is Maria Delores incidentally. I am reluctant to reveal this Mr. Dawson, and I want this left out of your report unless it is absolutely germane to proving what happened to my father," Carson said.

"Alright."

"My father and Maria had an affair. Clarisa found out about it. She didn't seem to care too much about it. My father swore to end it and gave Maria that little sports car to make it up to her, since he was ending the affair. It could be a motive for Clarisa. She actually told me directly once that she didn't care about it. She may be proving that, to herself, by not firing Maria. My father told me about this, he was puzzled as well," Carson said.

"Aaron said he didn't know much about your father's business affairs since your father would not talk to him about business," Matt said.

"Aaron has thrown a great deal of my father's money down rat holes. He has this idea that he knows how to set up a nightclub and make money with it. He has tried numerous times, losing every penny and then some. A couple tries ago my father refused to help him any further. He had to take bankruptcy on that one. His problem was that he would rather be a night club patron than a manager," Carson said.

"Is he in financial trouble now?"

"I think Clarisa is giving him an allowance."

"I have an appointment this evening with the eye witness to the hit and run and I met the police detective on the case," Matt said.

"Did the detective cooperate?"

"Yes, he was generally helpful, though I think he is relying on a body shop reporting a car with damage caused by the hit and run."

"Alright, continue to keep me informed."

The Tanurack Gentlemen's Tennis Club was located out in the Presidio area of San Francisco. It was four thirty when Matt turned in at the substantial gate proclaiming the establishment's name and went up a short winding drive to the parking lot. The lot consisted of a simple paved rectangle area with cars parked in four rows across and one row up next to the entry walk leading to the clubhouse. Matt noted the member's only sign, found a parking spot and walked around all around the parking lot. Finally he went up the walkway. On the left of the club house entrance he saw the club manager's office.

Terrance Withers was seated at his desk as Matt knocked on the open doorway.

"Can I help you?" Terrance said.

"Yes, thanks," Matt advanced up to the desk and handed Withers a card.

"I've been hired by Carson Ashton to look into the death of his father, Devin Ashton," Matt said.

"Oh yes, awful for the club and for the Ashton family I'm sure, what can I do for you?"

"I would like a file from your computer of your club members and a list of the court sign ups for the night of the hit and run," Matt said. He already had a copy of the list, but if he could get a file it would save a lot of typing.

"We try to keep our membership confidential, Mr, aw…. Dawson," Terrance said.

"I can understand, but Mr. Ashton was killed here in your parking lot. I'm not a lawyer, Carson Ashton is, I'm sure he would have a more understanding feeling toward the club where he father was killed in a dark parking lot, if you cooperated with my investigation," Matt said.

"I see your point. I think the board would approve of releasing the information in this case," Terrance said.

One of the club employees walked by the office door. "Aimy, oh Aimy could you come in here a second. Aimy runs our computer system. Could you give this gentleman the information he needs? It's concerning that hit and run we had last

week. I told him he could have our membership list," Terrance said.

"I would expect you to keep that list confidential, Mr. Dawson,"

"Yes, sir," Matt said and he shook Terrance's hand.

Matt followed Aimy out to her desk. She sat down at computer and hit a few keys.

"Any chance you could give me a flat file of the member names and another on

the court assignments for the evening of the hit and run?"

"What's flat file?"

"Can you direct the output of your reports to a file instead of out to the printer?"

Matt asked.

"Yeah, sure."

"That's a flat file," Matt said.

"OK."

In a few minutes Matt had a floppy with the information he needed.

"Which way to the bar?" Matt asked Aimy.

"Down this hall, out to the terrace and it's on your left," Aimy said.

"Thanks, for your help, Aimy,"

Aimy flashed a smile and said, "No problem."

Matt entered the bar and scanned the room. He checked his watch. It was a few

minutes after five. One man in a green and white warm up suit with gray partially

bald hair looked up and smiled at Matt.

"Mr. Zoltang," Matt asked.

"Karl Zoltang," Zoltang said and stood up as he extended his hand.

"Thanks for seeing me, I would like to go over exactly what you saw the evening

Mr. Ashton was killed," Matt said.

"Yes, I'll try to help."

Matt took out a small notebook. "When did you first notice Mr. Ashton?"

"Not until after I had heard the car."

"OK, let's start with that," Matt said.

"I had put my bag in the trunk as I always do. I was parked on the rightmost row of cars as you go out to the parking lot, about half way down."

"Were you standing by your trunk?"

"No, I had come around to the driver's side and I fumbled with my keys, dropped them. I leaned down to pick them up and that is when I heard the car gun its engine and spin its tires for the first time. I stood up and looked down to the row of parked cars across the top of the lot," Zoltang said.

"Did you see that car then?"

"Yes, Mr. Aston was standing by his car, he was parked about half way across that first row there, he had his trunk lid up, putting away his tennis bag too, I suppose, and then the car spun around the corner and hit him with its right bumper. He flew forward and, oh God, it ran him over. I could see the right side of the car lift up as it went over him."

Zoltang paused and drank a sip of water.

"What did the car do?"

"Well, it was going pretty fast, the driver had to hit the brakes for the turn to the left, he didn't totally make it. He slammed up against some of the cars parked on the row I was on. The driver gunned the car again and sped past me, hit the brakes at the end of the lot, turned to the left and gunned it down the little drive to the main road."

"Mr. Zoltang, you said 'he'. Was the driver a man?"

"The window were heavily tented, I only got the briefest glimpse as the car speed past me."

"Could you close your eyes and try to recall that glimpse."

Zoltang closed his eyes and tried to concentrate.

"You know, I think it may have been a woman. There was a lot of hair, glasses and the collar was pulled up, but it may have been a woman," Zoltang said.

"Did you tell the police that?" Matt asked.

"No, I'm afraid I didn't, they never suggested I close my eyes and try to recall it."

"I'll pass that along. They may want to call you to confirm that. If you don't mind, I think it would help me if you and I went out to the parking lot and you showed me exactly where everything was," Matt said.

"Sure."

Both men left the bar and walked out to the parking lot. Zoltang led the way over to the far row of cars and about half way down.

"We are such creatures of habit, that's almost the same place I parked this evening. That's my car there. I was parked further down that night." Zoltang indicated a large black Chrysler.

"OK, from here you can see over the tops of the cars in the middle to any car coming around the corner. Where was Aston parked?" Matt asked.

"See that red Jag, he was there I think," Zoltang said. The Jaguar was parked almost in the middle of the row of cars closest to the club.

"Did the police take any evidence of the collision with the other cars in this row that night?"

"Yes, I think they have paint samples from a couple cars' bumpers."

"Now, Mr. Zoltang, what can you tell me about the car itself."

"Well, as I told the police, it was a General Motors product, one of those subdued colors, a sedan, late model."

"Chevrolet?"

"I don't think so. You know they all look so much alike now."

"Did you notice anything about the license?"

"No, I'm sorry, I should have done that but I was pretty startled," Zoltang said.

"You didn't even glance at the license plate?"

Zoltang shut his eyes again. "You know, I think I did, but it didn't have a plate,"

Zoltang said.

"Anything that you can remember about the car?" Matt asked.

"No, not really, it was a standard shaped car, sorry."

"If I could have a minute or two more, let's go back to the bar and I'd like you to

look at a few pictures."

"OK, but my tennis match is in a few minutes," Zoltang said.

They went back to the bar and Matt had brought along the book he had purchased at

the bookstore. They found a table and Matt found the section on GM cars.

"Try to remember the grill on the car and see if you can find it in this group,"

Matt said.

Zoltang slowly paged through looking at the pictures of the General Motors

products.

"That's it, I remember the grill and headlight combination," Zoltang said.

Matt looked at the picture in the book. It was a 1997 Buick Century Limited.

"You're sure?" Matt asked.

"If it's not that one it's one that looks exactly like that one," Zoltang said.

"OK, that's great, thank you so much Mr. Zoltang, I'll pass this along to the

police. I'm sure they will want to verify what you've said but this really will help us

find the person who did this," Matt said.

"You know, thinking about it again, this had to be a purposeful act," Zoltang said.

"Yes, from what you've told me I think we are looking for a killer who chose the

car for her weapon," Matt said.

"There's my doubles partner, I have to go," Zoltang said.

"Thanks again."

Does Clarisa drive well enough to have done this? Matt asked himself.

Six

The next morning after a walk and a big breakfast in the hotel coffee shop, Matt set up his computer. He had some serious computing to do. First he created a database on his system of the members of the Tanurack Tennis Club. He made another of the members that had court assignments for the evening Aston was killed. Next Matt got on the Internet and found six hundred and twelve 1997 Buick Century Limited registered in Northern California. He then made a database of the cars registered to all the Tanurack Tennis Club members. Not one owned a Buick Century.

"There's water on the 'club member did it' theory," Matt thought.

Next, Matt extracted all the clubs and associations that Devin and Clarisa belonged to. From the Internet he created a file of all the people who belonged to these groups. This file was massive, so he had to edit out large groups such as the Northern California Automobile Association. He got the car registrations of all of these people. Finally he ran this massive list against those that had a 1997 Buick Century. Only one name popped out, Mrs. Carlotta Vasquez.

Matt ran a Profiler Report on Carlotta Vasquez. Carlotta belonged to the same country club that Clarisa did. Matt looked at the information on the Buick Century. It had been purchased from a dealer in Oakland only three weeks ago.

Matt picked up the phone and called Carlotta Vasquez. A maid answered.

"Vasquez residence."

"Could I speak to Mrs. Vasques, this is Matt Dawson."

"Sorry, she not here, can I take a message."

"Oh yes, she's at the club today," Matt said.

"Yes, she went to play golf again today."

"No thanks, I'll try to catch her at the club," Matt said.

Next he dialed the Lake Merced Country Club.

"Golf shop, please," Matt said when the operator answered.

"Golf shop."

"Yes, could you tell me when Mrs. Carlotta Vasquez's tee time is?" Matt asked.

"Just a moment."

"She's down for two fifteen."

"Thanks."

Well, all I need to do is find the course and the first tee before two fifteen, Matt thought.

Matt found the Lake Merced Country Club, taking State Route One south of the city. He parked in the guest parking lot and walked into the main lobby. He picked up a house phone and asked for a page for Carlotta Vasquez. After a few moments she came on the line.

"Mrs. Vasquez, my name is Matt Dawson, I'm looking into the death of Devin Ashton and I wonder if I could take a minute or two of your time before you tee off," Matt said.

"I don't know anything about that, but I suppose so, where are you?" Carlotta said.

"I'm in the lobby," Matt said.

"OK, I'm finished with lunch. I'll be there in a moment," Carlotta said.

Matt put down the phone and watched the entrance to the dining room. A Latin lady in her early fifties dressed in some spiffy golf togs came out the door. Matt went over to her.

"Mrs. Vasquez?" Matt asked.

"Yes, how on earth did you find me here?" Carlotta asked.

"It's my business to find people." Matt handed her his card.

"Maybe we could sit over here," Matt said indicating some chairs and couches set up in one area of the lobby.

"Mrs. Vasquez, do you know Clarisa Ashton?" Matt asked.

"Yes, of course, we play golf on a regular basis. I was so shocked to hear about her husband's death. I went to the funeral," Carlotta said.

"Did you know Mr. Ashton well?"

"Not really, I had been to a few functions at their home. Clarisa and I are also on the Bay Area Animal Rights Board of Directors, and I think Devin was at one or two of our functions as well. But I never knew him that well," Carlotta said.

"Mrs. Vasquez, I wanted to ask you about the car you purchased recently," Matt said.

"Really, is there something wrong with my new BMW?" Carlotta said.

"No, I was referring to your Buick Century, purchased a few weeks ago," Matt said.

"Don't be absurd, the last American car we had was back in the fifties, though they have improved greatly I understand."

"Could it have been purchased by someone in your family, in your name?"

"There's only me and my husband, and he drives an Infinity," Carlotta said. "We wouldn't have a place to keep another car. I had better get out to the first tee," Carlotta said.

"Alright, thank for your time," Matt said.

"Do you talk to the police?" Carlotta asked.

"Well, yes I'm working with Detective Kerns on this," Matt said.

"Maybe you could ask him to check and see if they have made any progress on my case," Carlotta said.

"OK, what case is that?" Matt asked.

"My wallet with all my credit cards was taken right from my locker, here at the club," Carlotta said.

"Oh, when was that?"

"It's been over a month now, I had attended a brunch at Clarisa's house that morning and then we came out for a round of golf."

"When did you notice your wallet was missing?" Matt asked.

"I looked for it after we finished our round. I went into the pro shop to get a few items and I couldn't find my wallet," Carlotta said.

"Could the purse have been taken at Clarisa's house?"

Carlotta looked at Matt as if he were certifiable. "Of course not. I haven't heard a single thing from the police."

"Did you lose your driver's license as well?" Matt asked.

"Yes, everything, it was so much trouble to get all those accounts closed," Carlotta said.

"I'll ask Detective Kerns to check the case's status for you."

"Oh, I'm being called on the tee, gotta go," Carlotta said and she hurried off.

Matt drove over the Bay Bridge to Oakland. He found the Very Best Auto Dealer out on Broadway. He pulled his rental car into the small customer parking space and got out. The very friendly used car salesman came promptly up with a big smile and "Yes sir, how can I help you? Care to trade your car in on something larger?"

"No, it's a rental car. Could you tell me where the manager is?"

"Hal should be in his office or on the inside floor, you sure I can't help you?"

"No, thanks," Matt said and he walked up to the doors leading to the inside showroom. Several late model cars where displayed and Matt headed for the little office with the sign 'Hal Brady, Manager' over the door.

Hal looked up as Matt stood in his doorway. "Yes sir, how can I help you?"

Matt handed him his card and said, "I would like some help on finding the salesman that sold a particular car a few weeks ago."

This must not have been the right thing to say because Hal suddenly seemed concerned.

"Is there something wrong with the car?"

"No, no. The driver of that car may have been involved with a hit and run."

"Oh, well, we can't be responsible for that."

"Certainly not," Matt said.

Hal relaxed a little and said, "I'll certainly try to help if I can."

"The car was a 1997 Buick Century Limited," Matt said.

"Within the last month, you said?"

"Yes."

Hal turned to his computer screen and hit a few keys. "Here's the one you probably are looking for. Sold over three weeks ago, Bob Goldman's sale."

"Is he here today?"

"Yeah, he's probably out on the lot somewhere or over at the coffee shop. Let me page him." Hal leaned over to the paging system speaker and microphone on his desk and said, "Bob Goldman, please come to the office, customer waiting."

Matt said,"I'm not interested in buying anything."

"I thought that might get him here quicker," Hal said. Hal knew that if he had said anything else Bob might choose to ignore the message.

After a few minutes Bob Goldman looked in at Hal's door. "You have something for me?"

"Yes, this fellow would like some information on a sale you made. I told him we would be happy to cooperate. They think the car was used in a hit and run."

"No kidding? Sure, come on back to my desk and I'll look up my records," Bob said.

Matt followed Bob back to his office over in the corner of the show room.

"So which car was it and when was it sold?"

"It was a 1997 Buick Century Limited sold just over three weeks ago."

"Yeah, I remember that one, little Mexican lady with the sun glasses?"

"I don't know, that what I'm trying to find out," Matt said.

Bob scanned down a desk drawer file filled with sale's contracts.

"Here it is, Mrs. Carlotta Vasquez, the car only had eight thousand miles on it."

"You remember the woman that bought the car?"

"You always remember the ones that drop from the sky. She just drove up in her little red Miata, got out and started walking down the line. We had the Century out on the end of the front row that day. It was a real cream puff," Bob said.

"She drove up in a Miata?"

"Yeah, I asked her if wanted to trade it in, but said she needed a nice family sedan, nothing too 'garish'."

"She used the word garish?"

"Yeah, that did seem strange, but she looked over the Buick and said it would be fine."

"How did she pay for the car?"

"That was unusual as well, she paid in nice new crisp one hundred dollar bills," Bob said.

"Could you think back and carefully tell me what she looked like," Matt said.

"I have her name."

"I know, but Mrs. Carlotta Vasquez says she did not buy the car."

"Oh. Well, she kept on her sunglasses both times she was here," Bob said.

"She came twice?"

"The first time she paid for the car and the next time she came to pick it up," Bob said.

"What was she wearing?"

"It almost looked like a golf outfit, slacks, colorful long sleeve shirt and a straw hat. The kind you see women wearing on a golf course," Bob said.

"What was her coloring?

"Well, she was Mexican, oh sorry, Latin, rather dark skin, black hair. I couldn't see the eyes because of the sun glasses," Bob said.

"How old do you think she was?" Matt asked.

"It's hard to tell, she had nice figure, but she kept the glasses and hat on, I would have to say late thirties maybe."

"Did she sign a contract?"

"Yes, here is a copy," Bob said.

Matt scanned down to the signature line. It was signed Carlotta Vasquez, with something of a flourish.

"Did she show an ID?" Matt asked.

"Yes, we have to get that since we are acting for the state in registering the car," Bob said.

"What did she show you?" Matt asked.

"I think it was a driver's license."

"I'll need a copy of the contract," Matt said.

"Sure." Bob stepped out of the office and came back in a few minutes and handed Matt the copy.

"The lady came the first time in a Miata, how about the second time to pick up the car?"

"I don't really know. She just walked into the showroom. Probably took a cab or something," Bob said.

"How did the woman talk?" Matt asked.

"Nothing special, a slight accent," Bob said.

"Did the car you sold her have a license plate?" Matt asked.

"No, it wasn't registered. We had to send in for a new one," Bob said.

"Thanks, you may be contacted by the police to go over again what you told me, this should help tracking the hit and run down."

"OK, and if you're in the market for a clean used car, I can look after you," Bob said.

"Thanks," Matt said and he headed back to San Francisco.

The next morning Matt returned to the police station and found Detective Kerns on the phone again.

"Have to go, see you later this evening," Kerns said after Matt sat down beside him. He hung up the phone.

"Mr. Dawson, you look as if you have some news," Kerns said.

"Yes, I've found out a couple of things," Matt said.

"Like what?"

"I think I have identified the car that was used to kill Mr. Ashton," Matt said.

"Really, how can you be sure?"

"Was the car color 'Champagne'?" Matt asked.

"Let me see," Kerns brought out the thick Ashton file and searched down until he brought out the report he was looking for.

"Yes, the analysis of the color of the paint from the bumpers that were hit by the perpetrator's car was a 'Champagne' used by General Motors."

"Here is a sales contract for the car, a 1997 Buick Century Limited. The color is Champagne," Matt said.

"Why do you think that this is the one?"

"I had a talk with the eyewitness, Karl Zoltang, showed him pictures of various late model GM cars. He's certain now, that it was a 1997 Buick Century Limited. He specifically remembers the grill."

"He only told us it was a GM product," Kerns said.

"He also said the car did not have any license," Matt said.

"Really?"

"Also, he now thinks the driver was a woman."

"I'm going to have to talk to Mr. Zoltang," Kerns said.

"I told him that you would probably want to verify everything he had said again," Matt said.

"If it was that make and model, how do you know it's this specific car?" Kerns asked.

"I took all the groups that the Ashton's belonged to and attached their car registrations to a database. Then I ran that database against all the Buick Century registrations. Only one name matched the criteria," Matt said.

"What, are you a computer expert?" Kerns asked.

"I suppose I would qualify as something like that," Matt said.

Kerns looked at the car sales agreement. "Did you find the car?"

"No, the lady whose name is on that document says she did not buy the car," Matt said.

"It was only purchased a few weeks ago, did it have a license?" Kerns asked.

"No, I found the salesman that sold the car, over in Oakland," Matt said.

"Did he remember the buyer?"

"Yes, he said it was a Latin woman, arrived initially at the car dealer's in a red Miata," Matt said.

"Does this Carlotta Vasquez drive a Miata?" Kerns asked.

"No, but Maria, Mrs. Ashton's maid does," Matt said.

"Is it red?"

"Yes, I checked the registration," Matt said.

"How do you leap from Mrs. Vasquez to Maria, the maid?" Kerns said.

"Could you check a complaint Mrs. Vasquez filed a few weeks ago, a theft?" Matt asked.

Kerns swung around and hit a few keys on his computer station. He checked the name on the sales contract once and brought up the record.

"She reported her wallet missing a few weeks ago," Kerns said.

"I talked to her about that and she said she had been at the Ashton's home earlier for a party that day. Then they all went to the golf course. She missed her wallet after they had finished golf, so she thinks it must have been stolen at the country club," Matt said.

"Your thinking there is a possibility that Maria took the wallet while Carlotta was at the party at the Ashton's house, used her Miata to drive over and buy the car," Kerns said.

"I hadn't taken it that far," Matt said.

"Why would Maria want to kill Devin Ashton?" Kerns said.

Matt remembered his instructions from his employer, Carson Ashton. Don't sully the memory of his father unless it is required to solve the case. This would probably qualify.

"Maria and Devin Ashton had an affair. Mrs. Ashton found out about it, Devin broke it off with Maria. In fact, he gave Maria the little red car as a peace offering," Matt said.

"My, you do uncover a lot of information. That could be a motive for murder, Latin's do have tempers," Kerns said.

"How did the car buyer pay for the car?" Kerns asked.

"Crisp one hundred dollar bills," Matt said.

"Where would Maria get the money?" Kerns asked.

"Also, where was Maria on the day the car was purchased?" Matt asked.

"And the key question, where is the car now?" Kerns asked.

"Could you check your computer and see if you have anything on this car? I once had a case where the car we were looking for was in the police impound lot all the time," Matt said.

"Sure." Kerns swung around and pecked away on his keyboard for a while.

"Bingo. There is an open traffic ticket on this car," Kerns said.

"What's the problem?"

"Parking in a handicapped space on …, the day after Devin Ashton was run down," Kerns said.

"Could I get a copy of that?" Matt asked.

Kerns clicked the print button, stepped across the hall and came back with a copy of the traffic violation.

"I believe it's time to talk to Maria." He shuffled down through his Ashton file, "Maria Delores."

"Would you mind if I came along?" Matt asked.

"Alright, it's your leads that are pointing to her. Sure, meet me here in the morning at nine and we'll head out," Kerns said.

Seven

Matt and Kerns drove to the Ashton house in Pacific Heights with in the detective's plain cover police car. They rang the bell and after several minutes Maria opened the door.

"Yes?"

Kerns held up his badge. "Maria Dolores? I'm Detective Kerns. I would like to ask you a few questions."

Maria looked flustered. "About what?"

"Just a few routine details to clear up concerning Mr. Ashton's death, can we come in?" Kerns asked.

Matt and Kerns moved past Maria into the entry hall. Clarisa was coming down the stairs.

"Who is it Maria? Oh, it's you Detective Kerns, and Mr…."

"Dawson, Matt Dawson," Matt said.

"Nice to see you again. Detective Kerns, do you have some word on the hit and run driver?" Clarisa asked.

"No Ma'am, we had a few questions for Maria here," Kerns said.

"Oh, well, you can use the living room if you like. I was going to get some coffee. Would either of you care for some?"

In unison Matt and Kerns said, "No thank you."

Clarisa moved off toward the back of the house.

Matt and Kerns followed Maria into the living room. Maria sat in an overstuffed chair and Matt and Kerns shared a large couch.

Kerns pulled out a small notebook, "Now, Miss Dolores, I wonder if you could tell us where you were on the weekend before Mr. Ashton was killed?"

"I had that weekend off," Maria said.

"I see. Where did you go?" Kerns said.

There was a pause. "Nowhere in particular," Maria said.

"Could you be more specific, exactly what did you do on that weekend?" Kerns asked.

Maria gripped her hands together on her lap. She looked down for a second and said, "I was out of town."

"Really, where did you go?"

"Lake Tahoe."

"I see. Where did you stay while you were there?" Kerns asked.

"Why do you need to know this?" Maria asked.

"Miss Dolores, did you buy a car in Oakland that weekend?" Kerns asked.

Maria looked surprised, "No, how could I?"

"Maria, if you were in Lake Tahoe, and you stayed in a hotel, you can tell us which one. Then we can check the registration and this matter can be put aside," Matt said.

"I didn't stay in a hotel," Maria said.

"Where did you stay?" Kerns asked.

Maria looked away.

"Miss Dolores, I think we need to continue this down at the station. It shouldn't take long, but we need the answers to these and a few other questions. Let's go," Kerns said.

Matt and Kerns stood up. Reluctantly Maria got up and headed for the door.

"Matt, put her in the car and I'll tell Mrs. Ashton we're leaving," Kerns said.

Matt followed Maria out the door. She took her apron off and was carrying it. She was getting angry. Matt opened the back door to the car and went around to the other side and got in.

"What are you hiding, Maria?" Matt asked.

Maria refused to answer and just looked out the window. Kerns returned to the car and they drove back to the police station. When they arrived, they went up to the floor where Kerns had his office. They put Maria in a small conference room. Matt and Kerns went over to the water cooler and got a drink.

"She's acting guilty enough," Kerns said.

"She is definitely hiding something," Matt said.

"Wait here, until I check in with my Lieutenant," Kerns said.

Matt was sitting on bench in the hallway when Aaron Ashton came up the stairs. He saw Matt and came over.

"Where is Maria?" Aaron asked.

"She's in that conference room. Why are you here?" Matt asked.

"Clarisa told me that you had brought Maria down here. She hasn't done anything," Aaron said.

Kerns returned and asked, "Mr. Ashton, why are you here?"

"I'm concerned about Maria, I was telling Mr. Dawson, Maria hasn't done anything."

"Someone bought a car that we think was used to run down your father on the weekend before that happened. Miss Dolores seems to fit the description of that person," Kerns said.

"The weekend before my father was killed?" Aaron said.

"Yes," Kerns said.

"Maria was with me," Aaron said.

"With you?" Kerns asked.

"Yes, we spent the weekend at a lodge my family has at Lake Tahoe."

"Really? Could you wait a few moments here in the hall while we talk to Miss Dolores?" Kerns motioned for Matt to follow him. Matt and Kerns went into the conference room.

"Miss Dolores, do you know Carlotta Vasquez?" Kerns asked.

"I'm not sure, I think she may be one of Mrs. Ashton's friends," Maria said.

"A few weeks ago she had her wallet stolen," Kerns said.

"Well, I didn't steal it," Maria said.

"OK, Maria we need to know where you stayed in Lake Tahoe," Kerns said.

Maria looked down at her hands.

"Aaron Ashton says you were with him that weekend," Kerns said.

"Yes, I was. I didn't want to say because I already have had one problem like this with Mrs. Ashton," Maria said.

"Yes, we know about you and Mr. Devin Ashton," Kerns said.

"Were you angry about Mr. Aston breaking off with you, Maria?" Matt asked.

"I was hurt, of course. But Mr. Ashton gave me the car, and Mrs. Ashton let me keep my job. I didn't have too much to complain about," Maria said.

"Wasn't Mrs. Ashton angry with you?" Matt asked.

"She tried to act like it wasn't important to her. Maybe that's because she had her on thing going on the side," Maria said.

"What makes you think that?" Kerns asked.

"This guy who called her several times. She has a lot of calls but somehow this one was different. She seemed more excited when he called," Maria said.

"What was this fellow's name?" Matt asked.

"I can't remember exactly, some kind of silly name I think. He only used his first name. Maybe it was 'Woody'. She always dropped whatever she was doing to talk to him. She didn't always do that," Maria said.

"Maria, how did Aaron and his father get along?" Matt asked.

"Not very well, in fact Aaron was angry with his father for not helping him with his business," Maria said.

"What business is that?" Kerns asked.

"He is opening a new night club in North Beach," Maria said.

"Maria, have you ever bought a car in Oakland?" Kerns said.

"I have never bought any car, Mr. Ashton gave me the one I have," Maria said.

"On the night Mr. Ashton was killed, what exactly were you doing?" Kerns asked.

Maria looked down at her clasped hands again. "Aaron was in my room. We were making love most of the evening," Maria said.

"You don't know whether Mrs. Ashton was in the house or not, do you?" Matt asked.

"No, not really," Maria said.

"And Mrs. Ashton doesn't really know if you and Aaron were in the house as well," Kerns said.

Kerns gave Maria a pen and a yellow pad. "Could you jot down what you've said here this morning, about being in Lake Tahoe with Mr. Ashton, and about being with him in his room that night?"

Maria scratched away for a few minutes.

"Maria, I'm going to have your statement typed up and then we'll have it for the record," Kerns said. "Sit tight and we'll be back in a few minutes."

Matt and Kerns returned to the hall. Kerns went toward his office to get the statement typed up. In a few minutes he returned.

"Let's talk in here a few minutes, Mr. Ashton," Kerns said. Kerns opened the door to a second conference room. Aaron sat down and crossed his legs. He seemed relaxed.

"You and Maria are having an affair?" Kerns asked.

"I should think that would be evident," Aaron said.

"Where you in her room on the evening your father was killed?" Kerns asked.

After a slight pause, "Yes, I was."

"I understand you are starting a new business," Kerns said. "Would you mind telling me where you got the money?"

"Not that it's any of your business, but I got an SBA loan," Aaron said.

"You would have enough cash to buy a car if you needed one?" Kerns said.

"I don't know why you would say that, but yes, we have funding we are now using for the build outs for the club," Aaron said.

"Did your father help you get that loan?" Kerns said.

"No, that's a laugh. He wouldn't give me the time of day." Aaron suddenly looked upset. "I loved my father."

"OK, thank you for your cooperation, Mr. Ashton, you can take Maria home now if you want to or we will send her home in a squad car," Kerns said.

Aston stood up and walked wordlessly out to the hall. Kerns followed him and opened the door to Maria's conference room.

"Could you wait a moment," Kerns said.

He walked down the hall and returned with a sheet of paper.

"Read over and sign this and you can go, Maria," Kerns said.

Maria glanced over the paper and signed it. Matt and Kerns watched Aaron lead Maria down the stairs.

"I think they are in this together," Kerns said.

"What was that about the statement?" Matt asked.

"I wanted a sample of her hand writing. We'll compare that to the signature on the car sales agreement," Kerns said.

The next morning Matt was up early to go out to the airport. He braced against the propeller wash as Frank swung the Beechcraft Bonanza around and into a parking spot at the SFO Executive Terminal. Frank cut the engine and climbed down. He handed Matt his gear and shut up the airplane.

"Thanks for coming up, Frank," Matt said.

"Haven't got it all figured out yet, huh?" Frank said.

"Maybe I have, but it's not coming out as we expected."

Frank arranged for the Bonanza to be serviced and got into the rented Taurus next to Matt.

"So, how is it coming out?" Frank asked.

"I'd better go back and tell you how I got here," Matt said as he drove out to the main freeway into the city.

Matt told Frank about how he had gotten the hit and run eyewitness to identify the exact make and model of the car. Then he had used that and the Ashton's associations, and their cars to find out who knew the Astons and owned such a car. He told Frank how that had led to a friend of Clarisa's, Carlotta Vasquez and then to Very Best Auto Sales.

"Did you show the car dealer a picture of Carlotta Vasquez?" Frank asked.

"No."

"You say the person claiming to be Carlotta wore what looked like a golfing outfit?" asked Frank.

"Yep and a hat and sunglasses. She drove a car like Maria, Clarisa's maid. Carlotta's wallet had been stolen so this person had her ID. Here's a copy of the sales contract for the car. The San Francisco detective is matching the signature to that of the maid, Maria."

"Did you have Clarisa's hand writing compared to this contract?" Frank asked.

"No."

"How about Carllota's?"

"No."

"You didn't mention to the detective that you more or less started out to just find out how Clarisa killed her husband?" Frank asked.

"No, he likes the maid and Aaron for it, acting as a team for the deed," Matt said.

"Carson Ashton is not going to be happy about all this," Frank said.

"That's why I wanted you up here, to help me ring this out more before I bring Carson up to date," Matt said.

"What else have you got to look into, besides those points I brought up earlier," Frank said.

"Yeah, we can check those out, let me see something," Matt pulled off the freeway and into a gas station.

He got out, opened the trunk and took out his briefcase. He sat down in the car again and searched for the police report about the Buick.

"This citation was made on the Buick Century on the day after Devin Ashton was killed," Matt said.

Frank read though the document, "Parking in a handicap zone. This is important?"

"You never know, let's see if we can find this place," Matt said.

Matt pulled out a detailed map of San Francisco Bay area. They found the location on the map and Frank plotted a course to get them there.

The address was in the city of San Mateo, south of the San Francisco Airport they had just left. The location detailed in the complaint was in front of Harry's Bayview Deli in a small shopping center.

Matt pulled up and parked in front of the deli. Both he and Frank got out of the car.

"What in the world was that car doing parked here?" Frank asked.

Matt shrugged. You could in fact see the South Bay out to the east of the little parking lot. As they stood gazing out in that direction, a police car came slowly up. Matt signaled for the cop to stop. The car pulled to a stop and Matt went around to talk to the officer.

"May I help you, sir?" the officer said.

"Yes. I'm investigating a case that involves a ticket written on a car in this parking lot," Matt said.

"Yeah, may I see some ID?"

Matt showed him his driver's license and gave him a card.

"Was it your car?" the officer said.

"No, here's a copy of the complaint report," Matt said and he handed him the copy.

"Oh yeah, I remember this one, I was riding with Bill Himes when we posted this, really strange," the officer said.

"Why is that?"

"Well, the car was here all night. We came by around two AM the first time. That convenience store over there has the record as the most robbed business in the Bay Area. We've been making random passes to try to get them out of the running for that honor," the officer said.

"When did you see it again?" Matt asked.

"We made one last pass on our shift that night. Must have been seven AM or so, it was then we noticed that it was parked in a Handicapped parking spot. We had come through here so often without getting anything done. We took the opportunity to write that one up."

"Notice anything else about the car?" Matt asked.

"No, late model with a temporary tag, it was gone the next evening when we made our first pass in here."

"Ever catch a robbery in progress?" Matt asked.

"No."

"OK, thanks a lot officer," Matt said.

"You bet," the officer said and drove slowly on.

"The killer left the car here overnight, Frank," Matt said.

"Yeah, probably in a hurry, didn't notice the handicapped parking," Frank said.

"Let's see how long it takes us to get from here back to the Ashton's house in Pacific Heights," Matt said.

Matt pulled out the map again and tried to plot the fastest way to the north east part of the city.

"Why does it matter how long it took?" Frank asked.

"The hit and run happened at about nine that night, the police were at the Ashton house at eleven," Matt said.

"Let's get out to 101, go north to Geary, over to about Divisadero and go north," Frank said.

They got back into the car and with Frank navigating, and keeping track of the time, drove up into the city and into the Pacific Heights district.

"That's the Ashton house," Matt said.

"It's over twenty one miles, and it took us thirty one minutes," Frank said.

"Probably could have done it faster around nine or ten at night," Matt said.

"Let's check the time from the tennis club to the parking lot," Frank said.

Matt drove over to the Tanurack Tennis Club and around the parking lot.

"This is where Devin Ashton was killed," Matt said.

Frank marked the time and they drove back out and over to 101 again and down to San Mateo. That proved to take twenty-six minutes.

"The club is about six miles closer to San Mateo," Frank said.

"Someone starting from the Ashton house could drive to the club, do the deed, come back here to this little parking lot, switch cars and return back to the Pacific Heights house, all in time to meet the police at the door," Matt said.

"Why all the way down here though? And where is the car that was parked at the lot now?" Frank asked.

Once again they got out of the car. Matt looked out over the parking lot. The mall consisted of convenience store, a deli, a thrift shop, a video store and several empty retail spaces.

"I don't know," Matt said.

They climbed back in the car and headed back to the Comfort Inn by the Bay.

Eight

After Frank had checked into the hotel, he and Matt met in the hotel coffee shop.
They ordered some lunch after Frank had given the waitress the third degree about
the daily special, Mountain Trout.

"There is one other base I want to touch," Matt said.

"What's that?"

"Betty Garrison," said as he pulled out a Profiler Report from his sports coat
pocket.

"Who was she again?" Frank asked.

"She worked at Aston Ventures and was on the hike when the first Mrs. Ashton
was killed," Matt said.

"What is she going to say differently now?" Frank asked.

"Devin Ashton is dead and she is now retired," Matt said.

Matt pulled out his cell phone and called Betty.

"Hello."

"Is this Ms. Betty Garrison?" Matt asked.

"Yes."

"I wonder if you could give me a few minutes of your time, I'm a private
investigator and I'm looking in to Mr. Devin Ashton's death."

"Why yes, I don't know how I could help, I hadn't seen Mr.Ashton for over six years,"
Betty said.

Matt verified her address and set up an appointment for four o'clock. Betty
Garrison lived in an apartment in the Sunset district, not far from Ocean Beach on
the western boundary of San Francisco and south of the Golden Gate Park. Betty
ushered Matt and Frank into her small living room.

"You have a nice location here," Matt said.

"Yes, I always have wanted to be near the ocean. I also love to walk up to the park as well," Betty said.

"Ms Garrison, I understand from reading a detectives report from 1980 that you were on the hike when the first Mrs. Ashton had the accident."

"Goodness, yes, that was a long time ago," Betty said.

"Glen Easton said in his report that he thought you were reluctant to talk about what had happened," Matt said.

"I suppose I was. I was still working at the company. Mr. Ashton was quite close to Clarisa. I didn't want to say anything," Betty said.

"What did you see?" Matt asked.

"Well, I can't be sure. That's the main reason I didn't say anything. It seems like Clarisa was standing directly behind Mrs. Ashton. She moved her hands quickly down to her sides as I came around the big rock on the trail that morning. It may have been that I just startled her," Betty said.

"She was in the act of pushing the first Mrs. Ashton over the edge?" Matt asked.

"I can't be sure. It's always bothered me. It would have been my word against Clarisa's. She was the Executive Secretary. I was a rather new employee, a manager, but still I wasn't too secure in my job."

"At the time, did anyone ask you about this?" Frank asked.

"That's the surprising thing. No one asked me about anything. I don't think anyone suspected any foul play, and I wasn't sure about anything like that either," Betty said.

Betty stared down at the coffee table for a few seconds. Matt and Frank had run out of questions. Matt was thinking that it was incredible that someone would keep something like this a secret.

"What does this have to do with Mr. Ashton's death?" Betty asked.

"We have been looking into Clarisa Ashton's past. Mr. Ashton's accidental hit and run is just the last in a long string of 'accidents'," Matt said.

They left Betty's apartment after Matt asked her to write out what she remembered of that morning. She was to include all the qualifications she thought necessary and mail it to Carson Ashton's office. When they got back in the car, Matt called Detective Kerns.

"Kerns."

"Detective, this is Matt Dawson, I was wondering if you had checked with that used car salesman, Bob Goldman yet?"

"I went over there yesterday afternoon."

"Did you show him Carlotta Vasquez's picture?"

"Yes, and Maria Dolores," Kerns said.

"What did he say?"

"He couldn't be sure. It could have been either of them, since the woman had on a hat and sunglasses. For my money it was Maria. She would have a reason to hide her appearance," Kerns said.

"How about the hand writing on the contract, anyone match up on that?" Matt asked.

"Our expert can't be sure. We gave him both Mrs. Vasquez and Maria's sample but I think I have them now," Kerns said.

"How's that?"

"Aaron Ashton took twenty thousand dollars out of the bank on the Friday before that weekend. I think that's where the money for the car came from."

"Did you ask him about the money?" Matt asked.

"He said that he used it to gamble in Lake Tahoe," Kerns said. "No record of his losses, of course. What have you found out?"

"I went to the parking lot where the Buick was parked overnight. It's down in San Mateo. I talked to a police officer that confirmed that the car had been there from two AM until seven AM. It was gone the next evening," Matt said.

"The question is where is it now?" Kerns said.

"Yes, I also timed the drive from the tennis club to the parking lot and from the parking lot back to the Ashton's house," Matt said.

"And?"

"It took under an hour for the whole round trip," Matt said.

"The hit and run was at nine or so. We were at the Ashton's house at..." Matt could hear Kerns leafing through pages. "Here it is, eleven fifteen. Maria could have run down Mr. Ashton and have been back in plenty of time," Kerns said.

"Anyone in that house could have done it," Matt said.

"What, Aaron? The witness, who I also talked to again this morning, said it was probably a woman driving the Buick," Kerns said.

Matt let it pass. There were two women in the house.

"We're going back again to each of the most likely car repair facilities. I think something will break there eventually," Kerns said.

"OK, thanks, I'll let you know if I turn up anything," Matt said.

"Sounds like you failed to mention Clarisa again," Frank said.

"He wouldn't hear of it unless I have something to back it up with," Matt said. "I guess I can't wait any longer to talk to Carson about this."

Matt called Carson and set up a meeting to go over what he had found out. Frank and Matt returned to Carson's office at ten AM the next morning. They were immediately shown into the conference room. Carson Ashton joined them and they all sat down.

"I got a call from that detective this morning. He wanted to know about my brother's relations with my father," Carson said. "What is he thinking?"

"He has a theory that your brother Aaron teamed up with the maid, Maria, to run down your father," Matt said.

"What? Aaron wouldn't have the guts to do that."

Matt went carefully through all the steps that had uncovered the Buick and the woman that had bought the car. He filled Carson in about his brother's affair with the maid and how he had drawn out twenty thousand dollars for an alleged trip to Lake Tahoe.

"We do have a house on Lake Tahoe and Aaron has a gambling problem," Carson said.

"Did you know about him and Maria?" Matt asked.

"No, but it doesn't surprise me. I might give some of this credence except I know Clarisa did it," Carson said.

"The trick is to prove it," Frank said.

"Isn't it rather surprising that Aaron could get an SBA loan?" Matt asked.

"I heard about that and did some checking. That was Clarisa's doing. She got to a bank officer and is actually standing behind the loan, herself," Carson said.

"Why would she do that?" Frank asked.

"I can't explain it. She has always liked Aaron best. She thinks he is less of a stuffed shirt than the rest of us, I guess," Carson said.

"Maybe she senses that you have your suspicions and she wants to reduce the number of family members that are out to get her," Frank said.

"When is the will to be probated?" Matt asked.

"Next week," Carson said.

"The police checked the maid's and Mrs. Vasquez's hand writing against the signature on the sales contract. Here is a copy of that contract. Do you know a handwriting expert that we can use to compare that to Clarisa's handwriting?" Matt asked.

"Yes, she sends me notes from time to time on managing her affairs. I have one expert I think is probably the best in the field," Carson said.

"You think it could have been Clarisa that bought the car?" Frank said.

"The car buyer was in a disguise, sunglasses, hat, and golfing clothes. She was supposed to look like Mrs. Vasquez," Matt said.

"Clarisa is not a Latin," Carson said.

"Makeup. She applied theatrical makeup to darken her skin and the sunglasses hid her blue eyes," Matt said.

"If Clarisa bought the car, where did she get the cash?" Frank asked.

"Mr. Ashton, could you check her bank accounts to see if she took out enough to buy that car?" Matt asked.

"Yes, I have access for most of her accounts," Carson said.

"Why, basically, is it that we think Clarisa did this?" Frank asked.

Carson gave him an annoyed glance. "Well, there has just been too many 'accidents' in her past," he said.

"Exactly. I think we can lay out that she had a motive to do this current crime, but I think what Frank is driving at is that we need to lay out a pattern here to get anyone to believe us," Matt said.

"Yes, you're right. Without knowing Clarisa's past, no one is going to believe that she could do this," Carson said.

"By the way, what kind of driver is Clarisa?"

"She has a top of the line Lexus sport utility that she tools around in like a maniac," Carson said. "The last time she drove me to the airport, I swore I wouldn't ever ride with her again."

"As I recall, her first husband also met with an accident. I think Frank and I should go over to Wyoming and see if we can put together a few more details on that. If I give you a report detailing all this, and particularly more information on how her first husband died, do you think that will be enough to convince a judge to give you an injunction?"

"I think so, can you leave tonight?" Carson said.

"We'll check the weather, and leave as soon as possible."

"I need to have that report in my hands early next week."

"Mr. Ashton, I have one other thing to report to you."

"Yes."

"I think it's possible that Clarisa killed your mother."

Nine

Frank and Matt got an early start for Wyoming, though they we starting behind the rest of the country, flying east into the sun. They quickly passed over the Sierra Nevada range and flew over the vast badlands areas of Nevada.

"Let's sit down in Salt Lake. I could use a rest stop and some breakfast," Frank said.

"We might as well top off the tanks while we're there," Matt said.

"It's frustrating when you know something but you can't prove it," Frank said.

"Without some proof, we can only suspect what Clarisa has done. I have a strong feeling that she is in fact, a serial killer," Matt said.

"How many people have had accidents in her life's journey?" Frank asked.

"Let's see, her first husband, the first boy friend in San Francisco, Amelia Ashton, and now Devin Ashton. What that, four?" Matt said.

"And no one has ever openly accused her of anything," Frank said.

"There's the Great Salt Lake," Matt said.

"Yep, have you on the ground in a few minutes, pardner," Frank said.

Frank expertly guided the plane into the Salt Lake City Airport landing pattern and made a flawless landing. Frank pulled up to a large fixed base operator and killed the engine. Matt arranged to have tanks filled and Frank sought out the comfort station. Matt found a phone and called Quincy.

"Are you on your way back?" Quincy asked.

"No, we are in Salt Lake City, heading for Cheyenne Wyoming," Matt said.

"How's the case coming?"

"I think we are making some progress. I need to send a report in this next week which may wrap it up from my end," Matt said.

"Is Frank with you?"

"Yes, I see him over there shooting the breeze with the coffee shop waitress," Matt said.

"Where are you going after Wyoming?" Quincy asked.

"Probably head back to San Diego," Matt said.

"Let me know when," Quincy said.

Matt joined Frank for breakfast and they got back on the Bonanza for the last leg to Cheyenne. The short hop over the mountains east of Salt Lake was bumpy but Frank veered off to the north and into the Great Divide Basin. It was more or less flat country all the way into Cheyenne.

"This is where most of the wagon trains came through," Frank said.

"Sky Harbor airport control at Cheyenne is on fourteen thirty-six," Matt said looking at the Jepperson Airport Directory.

Frank contacted the tower and they were on the ground at the Executive Terminal in fifteen minutes.

"Bags or counter?" Frank asked.

"You see to the airplane and I'll take the bags and get a car," Matt said. Matt got a car, put in the bags and picked up Frank from the fixed base operator's office.

"There's a good hotel north of the airport," Frank said.

"How do you know?" Matt asked.

"The gas lady told me."

"Can't go wrong then."

When they registered at the Fairfield Inn, Frank suggested they get a suite instead of two rooms, so that they would have more space to work in.

"You get two bedrooms with that?" Frank asked.

The desk clerk nodded and they stored their gear in the suite on the third floor, with a nice view of the airport.

"Time to get this research started," Matt said.

"I never liked that word in school. Where do we start?" Frank asked.

"Where would you start when you were in school?"

"At the library. I always hated the library."

Matt pulled out the city map he had picked up and found the Laramie County Library. After a few wrong turns they found the library and pulled into the parking lot.

Frank followed Matt up to the main desk where Frieda Holtman, Head Librarian, the little sign said, looked up over her horned rimmed glasses. Frieda was gray headed, overweight and looked to be in her mid fifties.

"May I help you?"

"Yes, Ma'am. I was wondering if you kept high school yearbooks?" Matt asked.

"Yes, which school, do you want?"

"Rogers High School," Matt answered. He had Clarisa's Profiler Report under his arm.

"Turn around and it's on the far back wall, off to your left," she said.

"Thanks," Matt said.

"What are we looking for?" Frank asked as they scanned down the shelves of the dusty books.

"Years 1955 to 1959, those were the years Clarisa was in high school," Matt said as he pulled four red covered books from the shelf.

"You start with 1955 and I'll start with 1959, you work up and I'll work down. See if you can find anything about Clarisa and anyone that might have known her," Matt said.

They found a table and began looking slowly through the books.

"Here she is as a freshman. Looks kind of glum," Frank noted.

A few more minutes went by while they looked carefully at the books.

"Here's something interesting. A picture of Clarisa and Jenny Paladora, they were officers of the Thespian Club," Matt said turning the book toward Frank.

Frank looked over Matt's shoulder as he turned to the next page.
"Ha, look at that," he said.

The picture showed Clarisa, on a stage with several other students. They were putting on a production of West Side Story.

"Yeah, Clarisa is playing Maria," Matt said.

"She seems to look quite Puerto Rican, too," Frank said.

"She has on a black wig and face paint. I guess they didn't worry too much about her blue eyes," Matt said.

"Was this training for later life?" Frank asked.

"Yeah, maybe. Look here's another reference to Jenny Paladora. She is on the stage also," Matt said.

Matt wrote her name down in his notebook. He continued to turn the pages. Toward the back of the book various informal shots were included seeking to show memorable little events that took place during the school year.

"Here's another picture of Jenny Paladora," Matt said.

The shot showed Jenny walking with a tall, handsome young man out toward the football stadium. The young man was identified as Bobby Bennington. The caption was 'Most loveable sweethearts'. Matt put Bobby Bennington's name in his notebook.

They finished looking through the books. The drama club pictures were the only ones that showed Clarisa with anyone else. Matt looked at Clarisa picture as a senior.

"She was a nice looking girl. I guess that's all we can get from these musty tomes," Matt said.

They put the books back on the shelves and turned to leave but were confronted by Frieda, the Head Librarian.

"You should have returned those to the check in desk. We like to return the books to the shelves ourselves," Frieda said.

"Sorry, I didn't know," Matt said.

"Did your mother attend Rogers?" Frieda asked.

"No, we are interested in Clarisa Wilkes," Matt said.

"Oh, yes, I remember her. I was at Rogers when she was there. My goodness that was ages ago," Frieda said.

"We found a picture of her and Jenny Paladora. Did you know her as well?" Matt asked.

"Yes, I wasn't in their inner group or anything but we all knew about the trouble between those two," Frieda said.

"Really, what trouble?" Matt asked.

"It was over Bobby Bennington."

"How's that?"

"Well, Bobby and Jenny broke up. Jenny was crushed. Bobby started going with Clarisa. Some say because she gave him what he wanted, if you know what I mean," Frieda said.

"I think so, but what do you mean?" Matt said.

"Heavens, here I am gossiping about things so long ago," Frieda said.

"It is important that we find out as much as possible," Matt said.

"It can't hurt now, I suppose. There was talk that Clarisa got pregnant," Frieda said.

"Really?" Matt said.

"Yes, she was out of school for a month or so. Some say it was to get over an abortion. That was really a shocker in those days," Frieda said.

"Do you know where Jenny Paladora is now?" Matt asked.

"She's a lawyer, best female lawyer in Cheyenne they say," Frieda said.

"How about Bobby Bennington?" Matt asked.

"He had an accident shortly after all this happened. He never even got to graduate from high school. What a tragedy," Frieda said.

"An accident?" Frank asked.

"Oh, yes... a real tragedy I don't remember exactly what happened, but we all were so saddened. It was probably the first experience with death for many of us. Got to get back to the counter," Frieda said.

Matt thanked Frieda and he and Frank walked back to the car.

"Ring up another 'accident' in Clarisa's life," Frank said.

"Really unhealthy to be around her alright," Matt said.

The next morning the first stop was the office of the Wyoming Tribune-Eagle. The sign above the receptionist's desk said the Wyoming Eagle was the oldest newspaper in Wyoming.

"We'd like to look through the archives," Matt said to the clerk at the desk.

"Alright, please fill in this form and the archive room is on the second floor, third door on your left. Did you know you can access our archives from the Internet?" the young lady asked.

"Really, thanks," Matt said.

On the second floor a group of microfiche readers and a desk were in front of the microfiche storage units. Off in the corner was a computer station providing Internet access. Matt headed directly for the computer station, and brought up the Tribune-Eagle archive query screen.

"You could have done that from our hotel room," Frank said.

"Or from home on my boat. I'll get a start with this and then we can go to the microfiche," Matt said.

Matt searched for 'Dudley Haines' and 1966, the year of the rodeo accident. The search yielded two hits. Matt brought up the first article on Haines' death. He scanned through it. It said the rider was killed while he had just started a bull-riding event, when the cinch on his saddle came apart, throwing him in the path of a rider on another horse. The article gave the name of the deputy sheriff investigating the accident. The second article simply rehashed the first and stated that the death had been ruled an accident. Matt wrote down the name of the deputy sheriff.

Frank wandered around and finally stood by the desk passing the time of day with the microfiche clerk. Frank saw Matt jotting something down and came over.

"What did you find?" Frank asked.

"Just the name of the deputy that investigated Clarisa's first husband's accident," Matt said.

Matt started a search on 1959 and Bobby Bennington. Again two hits. The first article detailed how the Roger's High School Junior was hit and killed by a 1955 blue and white Chevrolet. Two witnesses agreed on the car description and the city police were searching for the car. The accident happened in front of a small malt shop only two blocks from the high school. No one could identify the driver of the car. The second article told that Bobby's father, Terrance J. Bennington, President of the First National Wyoming Bank, was posting a ten thousand-dollar reward for information leading to the arrest of the hit and run driver. Also, the story added that a stolen car might have been used to commit the crime.

"This sounds familiar," Frank said as he read over Matt's shoulder.

"Back in those days, more people left their keys in the car, so Clarisa might have been able to steal one," Matt said.

"They never mention finding the car," Frank said.

"Just like now. Let's see if we can find this deputy sheriff that handled the first husband's accident," Matt said.

Matt and Frank returned to their hotel suite and Matt set up his computer and ran a Profiler Report on Carey Burton, a Laramie County Deputy Sheriff in 1966 and on

Jenny Paladora. Mr. Burton now lived at a retirement home off highway 30 in

Cheyenne. Matt called and asked if it was all right to come out to talk to Mr. Burton.

"Sure, I know he'd like some company," the person at Mountain Towers said.

Matt and Frank easily found the Mountain Towers and were given Mr. Burton's

room number at the front desk. Mr. Burton's door was open. He was sitting in his

recliner, watching a baseball game.

Matt knocked on the door jam and asked, "Mr. Burton, could we speak to you for

a few minutes?"

At first Burton didn't respond, even though the sound on the TV was off, but he

didn't seem to hear. He noticed Matt at the door and reached to his ear to turn on

his hearing aid.

"What's that?"

"Mr. Burton, could we speak to you for a few minutes?" Matt repeated.

"Sure, glad for some company, come on in."

Matt and Frank entered and pulled up some side chairs.

"You fellows follow the Rockies?" Burton said.

"No sir, we're from San Diego," Matt said.

"Padres fans huh? They had some good teams once. They went to pot ever

since Tony Gwynn has been out of the picture," Burton said.

"Yes, sir. My name is Matt Dawson, and this is my friend Frank Pullen. We're

here trying to get some further information on a case you handled when you were a

deputy sheriff," Matt said.

"Yeah, I was a deputy almost thirty years. Handled probably a thousand cases. I

don't see how I could remember any particular one," Burton said.

"This one may have been unique," Matt said.

"Yeah, how's that?"

"In 1966 you handled the case of the rodeo cowboy that was killed when the girth on his saddle came loose," Matt said.

"Oh, yeah, I do remember that one. Strange situation. Never heard of that happening before or since. I always had a feeling something was rotten there, but I couldn't prove anything. Oh, and the girth didn't come loose, it came apart," Burton said.

"As if someone had partially cut it?" Matt said.

"I couldn't be sure. All the cowboys always kept close control of their own saddles, but it sure looked to me like it had been cut some," Burton said.

"Did you talk to the cowboy's wife?" Frank asked.

"Yeah, I think I did. Real pretty little thing she was. Didn't seem too upset about the whole thing," Burton said.

"Did you tell anyone about your suspicions?" Matt asked.

"Yeah, I told the sheriff, but he didn't want to drag the thing out," Burton said. "We couldn't figure who would have wanted him dead or anything. He was an average rodeo cowboy, never earned too much. Won now and again, barely made a living. We didn't know how to prove that the cinch was cut."

"Did you check for life insurance?" Matt asked.

"Yeah, I did, the wife got only ten thousand I think," Burton said.

They thanked Mr. Burton and returned to the parking lot.

"No one ever suspects her of anything," Frank said.

"Until now," Matt said.

Ten

As they sat in the parking lot, Matt consulted his Profiler Report on Jenny Paladora, pulled out his cell phone and dialed her office.

When she came on the line Matt said, "Ms. Paladora, my name is Matt Dawson. I'm looking into the early days of Clarisa Wilkes Ashton. I understand that you knew her in high school. I wonder if you would have a few minutes so that we could talk about that?" Matt asked.

"My calendar is full this afternoon, but I could spare you a few minutes in say half and hour, is that too soon?" Jenny asked.

"We'll be right over," Matt said.

They parked behind the small office building only a few blocks away from the state capitol building, and easily found the office on the second floor.

The receptionist asked them to wait for a few minutes. Finally she showed them into Jenny Paladora's office. Jenny had her college degrees prominently displayed on the wall off to the side of her desk. Jenny Paladora was a fiftyish woman, only slightly overweight and a pretty oval face and jet black hair. She had a large yellow ribbon in her hair that somewhat feminized her expensive looking business suit. Jenny came around the desk with a big smile and a lovely low voice.

"Hello, I'm Jenny Paladora. Sorry to keep you waiting but I got a phone call I had to take."

"Thanks for taking the time to talk with us, Ms. Paladora. My name is Matt Dawson. I'm a private investigator and this is my associate, Frank Pullen," Matt said.

"You know, I'm really out of time at this point. I wonder if you would consider getting a bite of lunch while we talk. There's a little Italian place next door where I usually go at noon."

Frank was hungry. "That would certainly be delightful."

Jenny grabbed her briefcase and they followed her down the back stairs. She led them out into a small alleyway and into the side door of Mario's Tratoria. Large jugs of Italian wine were stored on one wall. There were a dozen tables and a row of booths around the back of the room. The waiter smiled and waved to Jenny as she headed for her booth in the far corner. Matt stood aside to let Jenny slide in, but she held back.

"Would you mine sliding over? I like to be on the end. Us lefties need our room."

Both Frank and Matt quickly assented and moved into the booth.

After they had ordered Jenny asked, "Now, how can I help you?"

"I wanted to ask you about your years in high school with Clarisa Ashton," Matt said.

"Why are you interested?" Jenny asked.

"Mrs. Ashton's husband was killed. His son, Carson, has hired me to look into that. As a matter of routine we are checking out all the people in the case," Matt said.

"It's routine to fly out to Wyoming?" Jenny asked.

"Sometimes," Matt said.

"At one point Clarisa and I were quite close. Her brother keeps me informed of her doings. I can't believe I was once the confidant of one the world's richest women," Jenny said.

"Her brother David still lives here in Cheyenne?" Matt asked.

"Yes, we go out together occasionally. He has a chain of gift stores," Jenny said.

"You haven't seen her since she left Cheyenne?"

"No. Well, I did see her at the opening of an Indian art museum she had built here in Cheyenne. She was always fond of the Indians, I don't know why. She was always spouting the Indian's philosophy of life," Jenny said.

"Did you know Clarisa after high school?" Matt asked.

"She married a rodeo cowboy. I didn't pal around with her much after that but when he died I did get together with her. We had been close and I thought she would need some comforting. She had become pretty bitter about men. I guess the cowboy thought it was all right to smack her around. I think it was then that she started her plan," Jenny said.

"Her plan?" Matt asked.

"She decided if you were going to have to put up with a man you might as well get one that was rich. Sage advice, I suppose," Jenny said.

"So that was her plan?" Matt asked.

"Yes, she found out who were the richest men in America. Made a list of the eligible ones. That's when she decided that most of them lived in California and a lot of them in San Francisco," Jenny said.

"What's when she decided to move there?" Frank asked.

"Yes, she told me that I should do the same. The way it's turned out, she might have been right," Jenny said.

"When did she tell you all this?"

"I looked her up after I saw the piece in the paper about her husband being killed. I thought she would need someone to lean on. That's when she told me about this plan to change her life," Jenny said.

"Frank and I took a look at the Rogers High School Yearbook for 1959. We noticed that you were said to have a sweetheart named Bobby Bennington," Matt said.

"Yes, we were in love. At least I was. He was murdered," Jenny said.

"Murdered?"

Jenny opened her briefcase and pulled out a thick file and put it in front of Matt.

"You carry this around with you?"

Jenny laughed. "It is pretty heavy. Someday I'm going to find out who killed Bobby. Last weekend I had a conference to go to. I hadn't looked at the file for a while so I thought I would go over it one more time. In this file I have a copy of everything about the case. I spent four years as an Assistant District Attorney for Laramie County, to get my law career going, but also to try to find his killer. I got into trouble with the DA for spending too much time on this."

Matt opened the file and started leafing though the pages, "What more do you know at this point?"

"They found the car that killed him, only a few years ago," Jenny said.

Matt was sure that his ears pricked up. "Where was the car?"

"We have an area that was just something of a swamp. They cleaned it up to build the Frontier Day's Old West Park. We have a museum there and it's a nice area now. The lake was drained and that's where they found a 1955 blue and white Chevrolet. They have refilled the lake now," Jenny said.

"I read the report that said the witnesses agreed that was the make and model, but how can you be sure that it was the one?" Matt asked.

"The car was stolen. And the car serial number matched the one stolen from Reverend Parker's house," Jenny said.

"Reverend Parker?"

"He was a minister at the church Clarisa, Bobby and I went to. He would have Sunday evening parties for the Youth Church group. Things were straight laced in those days. Some parents would only let their teenagers go to church supervised parties. The reverend was a trusting soul. He told the officers that he usually kept the keys in the car. He was always losing things and he wanted to be able to take off if someone needed him," Jenny said.

"Do you have any idea, at this point, who took the car and ran Bobby down?" Matt asked.

"Since the car was taken from the reverend's home and the kids at his parties knew about the key thing and because several kids were jealous of Bobby, I think it was one of them," Jenny said.

"Jealous?"

"Bobby was the son of the richest man in town. He had a shiny new convertible, president of the senior class and a football star. He also wasn't the most humble person I've every known. I know several kids that hated him. He had a couple of run-ins with one or two of them. I've never been able to decide which one hated him enough to commit premeditated murder," Jenny said.

Matt took a sip of his water. "I understand Bobby Bennington dated Clarisa for a while."

"Yes, Bobby and I had a break up, over a stupid thing. We were starting to get back together when he was killed," Jenny said.

"You didn't have any problem because Clarisa was with Bobby for a while?" Matt said.

"In high school, boys and girls change partners a lot. Practicing for being adults doing the same things, I guess. But I really loved Bobby and I guess I always will. No, Bobby and Clarisa had a thing, and it was over. Both Clarisa and Bobby told me that much," Jenny said.

"Did you know that Clarisa was pregnant and got an abortion?" Matt asked.

"I heard that rumor. I asked Clarisa about it, she swore it wasn't true. She said she had hepatitis. It kept her out of school for a month or two," Jenny said.

"So, you and Clarisa are still friends?" Matt asked.

"We're friendly, but I don't move in her circles."

"Would you mind if I got a copy of some of your file, particularly about the 1955 Chevy and its recovery?"

"Sure. Actually, everything in that folder is a copy. Just keep it. I have my originals back in my file cabinet. But, why would you want that?" Jenny asked.

"Just trying to put in a complete report."

Their food came and the discussion shifted to the difference between living in Wyoming and California. Frank seemed to be very hungry.

Matt finished his sandwich. "Get enough to eat, Frank?"

Frank had downed a dish of lasagna. "Very delicious," Frank said patting his stomach.

Jenny finished and pushed back her plate. "I like a man who enjoys his food. Oh, I'm going to be late."

Matt paid the check and they went out the front of the restaurant.

"I want to thank you for your time Ms. Paladora, you've been quite helpful," Matt said.

"You're welcome and thanks for lunch. Would you keep me informed about anything you should find that relates to Bobby Bennington's death?"

"Certainly," Matt said.

Matt gave her his card and she scurried down the street.

When they got back to hotel suite, Matt returned a call from Carson Ashton.

"Have you found anything?" Carson asked.

"I believe we have. Yet another accident in Clarisa's past," Matt said.

Carson seemed agitated. "The judge has moved up the will probate. I need whatever you have quickly."

Matt glanced at his watch. "I'll have it to you by tomorrow morning. Give me your fax number again. I'll get the report ready and fax it to you," Matt said.

"Alright, do you have anything specific that can tie Clarisa into any of the accidents?" Carson said.

"Primarily the pattern, but I think I know where the car that killed your father is," Matt said.

"Outstanding. Get me the report as soon as possible," Carson said and hung up.

"That's going out on a limb," Frank said as Matt put down the phone.

"Yeah, it might be, but Clarisa seems to be a creature of habit," Matt said.

"So where is the car?" Frank asked.

"Let me have Detective Kerns check it out and we'll know for sure," Matt said as he dialed the number for the San Francisco Police Department.

When Kerns came on the line Matt said, "Good afternoon, detective. I think I have a place to look for the car that killed Devin Ashton."

"Yeah, where would that be?"

"You remember me telling you about checking out the parking lot where the car in question got a handicapped parking ticket?" Matt asked.

"Yeah, it was down in San Mateo, right?"

"If you go to that lot and look out to the east, you see the South Bay," Matt said.

"So?"

"I believe Clarisa killed another person here in Wyoming also by hit and run. That was many years ago. They couldn't find the car for years until they found it in submerged in a lake. I think the killer took the car, drove it into the South Bay, at some wharf or pier not too far from that parking lot. Could you poke around and see if there is a place where you could push a car into the water easily and have a short walk back to that parking lot?" Matt asked.

"You got it," Kerns said.

"Please give me a call on my cell phone if you find anything," Matt said.

"OK, will do," Kerns said and he hung up.

"Probably a good guess. But there may be many places there where you could run a car into the Bay," Frank said.

"Be optimistic, have faith in our public servants."

"How are you going to get that report done by the morning?" Frank asked.

"I'll start right now. Work through the evening if I have to," Matt said.

"Do you have a printer?"

"No."

"If you did, I could proof read it for you as you go," Frank said.

"That would help," Matt said.

"Be back," Frank said and he left the room.

Matt set up his computer and organized the material for his report. He decided to reference the first detective's report and include a summary of his findings. Matt set up a table of each of the accidental deaths, the date, relation to Clarisa, the type of accident and possible motive.

Bobby Bennington, 1959, ex boy fiend, hit and run, problem with an abortion?

Dudley Haines, 1966, first husband, cut saddle girth, abusive husband, insurance?

Howard Peterson, 1975, boy friend, drowned in bathtub, no marriage in sight?

Amelia Ashton, 1978, wife of plan target, pushed over cliff, make way for her as the next wife?

Devin Ashton, 1997, second husband, second hit and run? Problem with Devin having another woman? Just time for the next part of the plan?

Matt had a good portion of the report completed when Frank returned. He had gone to a computer superstore and bought a small printer. They hooked it up and soon had a copy of all the pages Matt had written.

"Let's get some dinner and then come back and finish this," Matt said.

"Yeah, I work better on a full stomach," Frank said.

When they had finished dinner they returned and Matt completed the report in another two hours. He printed out those new pages. Frank had read through the first portion and showed Matt the typos. By the time Matt had edited the first part of the report, Frank had finished reading the last part.

"We need some direct evidence, it's all circumstantial," Matt said.

"Yeah, we need the proverbial smoking gun, or in this case car, preferably with her prints on it," Frank said.

Matt changed the last portion of the report and connected the phone to computer and dialed Carson Ashton's office fax machine. It took ten minutes to send over the report.

"Is that a wrap?" Frank asked.

"I don't know what else we can do, particularly here. Let's head home in the morning," Matt said.

"Maybe that San Francisco detective will discover something. If he can find the car, then maybe there's something to tie Devin Ashton's murder back to Clarisa," Frank said.

"Hope springs eternal," Matt said.

Eleven

On the return trip to San Diego the next morning it was Matt's turn to take the
left seat. The flight was uneventful. The only notable event being the view as they
flew over the Grand Canyon. Frank slept most of the way. By the time they had
returned the airplane and got to Frank's car in the long-term parking, it was late
afternoon. Frank dropped Matt off at his marina and then headed for Coronado and
his condominium. Matt picked up his cat from the marina manager's office and
opened up his boat. Matt's boat was a Sun Odyssey 45.2. He had named her
Victoria, his mother's name. He had thought about naming it Juliann, the wife he
missed so much. He thought that would be too painful, to be reminded each day
that he had lost her. It hadn't worked, there wasn't a day go by that he didn't think
of Juliann. It was an elegant boat that boasted three cabins and two heads and an
excellent electronic package. She was a French built boat made by a company name
Jeanneau. It took a few minutes for the fresh air to flow through the cabin. He
checked his watch. He knew Quincey would be waiting to go on the air for her
evening news program. He called her cell phone.

"Hello."

"Quincey, I'm back," Matt said.

"What, here in San Digeo?"

"Yep, you about ready to go on the air?"

"Yes, I have three minutes," Quincey said.

"How about some dinner?"

"Great, shall I come over to your boat at ten or so?" Quincey said.

"Sure, we can eat here at one of the fish places," Matt said.

"See you then," Quincey said.

Matt had adjusted to eating later to fit in with Quincey's schedule. Several other
adjustments had to be made to be with a local celebrity. When they were together,

Matt could usually see one or two people staring at Quincey, possibly trying to place where they had seen her. It was novel and somewhat exciting at first but it became something of a drag.

Matt had just hung up from talking with Quincey when his cell phone rang.

"Matt Dawson."

"Mr. Dawson, this is Detective Kerns, San Francisco PD."

"What's the news, Detective?"

"We found it."

"The car?" Matt asked.

"Yes, it was submerged off the end of an abandoned pier. Someone had cut the chain on the fence to get through," Kerns said.

"Close to the parking lot?"

"Yes, only four blocks away."

"It's the same car?"

"A 1997 Buick Century Limited with damage to the right front which is consistent with hitting Mr. Ashton and then the run in with the other cars in the lot. The serial number matches the one sold in Oakland."

"Detective, that's great. Did you find anything in the car?" Matt asked.

"The car was totally submerged and the driver side window was down so there is no hope of any finger prints, but we did find a wig on the back seat floor," Kerns said.

"Did you check the gate for prints?" Matt asked.

"Yes, we may have one but it's not a good image."

"Detective, I think this implicates Clarisa Ashton. This is the same MO that was used on a classmate in her high school class in Wyoming. I will fax you a copy of my report on this. There are now five people in Clarisa's life that have had fatal accidents."

Matt could almost hear the wheels turning in Kerns' head. "Maria might be the one who used the wig as well. There is one other little development. I got a call from Clarisa Ashton," Kerns said.

"What did she say?" Matt asked.

"She now says she just remembered that she had called down to Maria to have her bring up another bottle of wine on the night Devin was killed, but she never answered. Clarisa, had to go down stairs and get one for herself," Kerns said.

"A convenient memory at this point. I think she is getting nervous and trying very hard to implicate Maria," Matt said.

"Let's see if we get anything out of this finger print," Kerns said.

"Will you match it against one of Clarisa's?"

There was another pause. "Yes, I will."

Matt felt a small sense of victory.

"OK, Detective thanks for the call. Please let me know what you find out about the finger print," Matt said.

Matt hung up and called Carson Ashton at his home.

Carson's wife answered and called her husband to the phone when Matt gave her his name.

"What have you found Mr. Dawson?" Carson asked.

"The San Francisco PD found the car that was used to kill your father."

"Really, where was it?"

"The killer had run it off an abandoned pier in San Mateo. It was the one purchased in Oakland by a woman wearing a wig," Matt said.

"Anything to connect it back to Clarisa?" Carson asked.

"There is a finger print from the pier gate they are looking at, and they found a wig in the car. They agreed to check the print against Clarisa's," Matt said.

"Can you fax me a note on this? I'll add it to the material I'm submitting in the morning," Carson said.

"Of course, I'll get it ready right now," Matt said.

"We should have a decision on my motion in the next few days. I'll call you and let you know what it is," Carson said.

"Alright, I'll wait to hear from you," Matt said.

Matt set up his computer and prepared an addendum to his report on Clarisa's accident-prone life. He emphasized the similarities between Devin Ashton's death and that of Bobby Bennington. It took less than a minute to fax the extra pages to Ashton's office. When he had finished he looked at his watch and saw it was time for Quincey to show up. Quincey and Matt had evolved a plan when they got together for dinner after one of Quincey's late night broadcasts. The TV station was only a short distance from Harbor Island and Marina Cortez where Matt kept his boat. So rather than have Matt find a parking place and be a stage door Johnny waiting for Quincey to finish up, Quincey would drive her Porche over to the marina parking lot where she would meet Matt at the entrance of the Barnacle Bill restaurant. They might have dinner there or at one of the several other seafood restaurants on the island.

Matt had just walked up to the entrance when he saw Quincey getting out of her car. He walked out to meet her. Halfway they met and embraced, Matt picking her up in his arms and they kissed.

"Glad you're home, sailor," Quincey said.

"I'll second that," Matt said.

"It seems like you've been gone a month."

"It's nice to have someone miss me."

Two blissful weeks went by with Matt and Quincey enjoying each other's company anew, with no word from Carson Ashton. Matt assumed that things must be progressing nicely. It was on a Saturday that they were once again on Harbor

Island. They decided on walking up to the end of the island and eating at Tom

Hamm's Lighthouse. The fish dinner was good and Quincey told Matt about some of

the news stories she had reported on during the last few weeks. A lady stopped by

their table and told Quincey how much she enjoyed seeing her on TV and asked for

an autograph. The only sour note came when Matt opened his mouth once too

often.

   "They had this wonderful sale on shoes at Nordstroms, I bought five pair,"

Quincey said.

    "Five pair, that was stupid. Why do you need five pair?" Matt said.

    "Matt, you never appreciate that I have to always look my best."

    "Sure, but how many pair of shoes do you have already?"

    "That's not the point. I'd spend a lot of money if it could give me an edge,"

Quincey said.

    "I think you went over the edge already."

He glanced at Quincey. "Oh, oh, went too far on that one," he thought.

Quincey gave him one of her icy glares.

They finished eating and strolled back to the marina. A full moon bounced its

reflection off San Diego Bay. When they got back to the parking lot Matt turned to

Quincey and said, "You want to stay over?"

    "I thought you would never ask," she said.

The next morning Matt awoke with Quincey next to him in the large rear cabin.

It was a large and comfortable bed though Matt usually slept in the forward cabin

when he was alone. This aft bed was more comfortable for two. DC, the cat, was

curled up at his feet. She usually tried to sleep up closer to Matt's head. She would

try to sneak up there in the middle of the night, thinking that all that purring made it

ok, but Matt had a strict rule. The cat was to be kept at the foot of the bed. He loved waking up to the boat's gentle movement and hearing the muffled sounds of the other boat's rigging clanging as the dawn breeze stirred them up. He could see the sky though the port directly above his head. Only the occasional takeoff roar of a jetliner from the neighboring San Diego International Airport disturbed this serenity. Sometimes, at this time of day, somewhere between waking up and being asleep he had his best thoughts about how to solve problems. But today was not for solving problems. Matt looked over at Quincey, she was a beautiful woman. She was moody at times and obsessed with her career, but a wonderful friend and lover. Quincey stirred and opened her eyes and smiled at Matt. She had a beautiful smile too. She spoke not a word but moved over on top of him and they made love once more to start the day.

After a while they went up to Maggie's Deli for a bagel and some coffee. The deli was a shop selling ice, soft drinks, beer, junk food and sandwiches. Outside the deli's door, overlooking the marina they had set up a few plastic tables and chairs. Maggie had a plan for a nice new deck to expand the eating area, but it never got beyond the concept phase. The seagulls acted as if it was their turf. A pair drifted over and landed on the embankment on the edge of the water. They began fussing with another earlier arrival, probably about territory. Matt and Quincey were finishing up when Matt's phone rang. It was Frank.

"I got a call from Martin Justin, he was upset," Frank said.

"How so?"

"He got a letter from Clarisa's attorney. She cut the Children's Cancer Hospital out of the will," Frank said.

"Maybe Carson's suit will stop that," Matt said.

"Further bad news. The judge dismissed Carson's suit. He said he saw was no direct evidence of any wrong doing on Clarisa's part. That she is backing the judge to be the county attorney had nothing to do with it," Frank said.

"Surely, this won't stand," Matt said.

"Martin says that Carson Ashton also got a letter indicating that he and sister Beth were not in the new will either. He is devastated. Martin thinks both he and Beth had borrowed heavily against the day that a good portion of the Ashton estate would be theirs," Frank said.

"Sounds like we are striking out on all fronts," Matt said.

"I don't know what else we can do," Frank said.

"It could all be reversed if Devin's murder is pinned on Clarisa," Matt said.

"Dammed hard to make that happen," Frank said.

"I guess I'll have to see what Carson wants to do now."

"Let me know if you hear from him," Frank said and he hung up.

"Not going too well, huh?" Quincey said.

"No, the black hats are winning this one," Matt said.

"Speaking of black, did you get your tux yet?" Quincey asked.

"Tux?"

"You haven't forgotten the Mayor's Charity Ball and Awards Dinner have you? I told you about it before you went to San Francisco, I got a new gown that I am dying to wear," Quincey said.

"Oh, yeah, right." He hated these formal affairs.

"Matt, you know how important this type of thing is for me. I like having a Tom Cruise kind of guy like you to take me to these things. That is why I put up with you," Quincey said.

"That's awfully nice of you."

Before she could respond Matt's phone rang again.

"Matt Dawson."

"Mr. Dawson, this is Carson Ashton. Have you heard about the law suit?"

"Yes sir, I understand the judge dismissed it. What are you going to do now?"
Matt asked.

"I need some additional facts. With that I'll file it again, see if I can't be sure it
goes to a different judge. I'd like you to continue to work on the case. Can you do
that?" Carson asked.

"Yes, alright, should I come back up there and follow up on what we know?" Matt
said.

"Clarisa isn't here anymore," Carson said.

"Where did she go?"

"She has been busy. First, she sold the company. She could do that as soon as
my suit was dismissed. She had been working on the deal every since my father
was killed. I didn't even know it. Did you know she has married again?" Carson
said.

"What?"

"It is astounding. She married a cowboy twenty years younger than she is,"
Carson said.

"How in the world did she meet a cowboy?" Matt asked.

"Apparently they met when Clarisa accompanied Aaron to a western bar where he
wanted to hear some singer that was performing."

"So where did the happy couple go?" Matt asked.

"Arizona. This fellow is a performer of sorts, he raises buffalo and puts on shows
with them or something," Carson said.

"What's his name?"

"Woody Montana."

"This is all mind boggling," Matt said.

"What could you do at this point?" Carson said.

"Maybe Aaron is the key now. How is the relationship between you and your brother?" Matt asked.

"Not good. He is angry with me because I supported my father in his position that led to Aaron having to declare bankruptcy. Why do you ask?"

"Clarisa called the detective on your father's case and said that she now remembers that she could not find Maria on the night that your father was killed. The detective thought that Aaron and Maria might have plotted together to kill your father. I might use Clarisa's new recollection to get Aaron to rethink his statement that he thought Clarisa was at home that night. Is he still living at the house in Pacific Heights?" Matt asked.

"No. He has moved to Phoenix with Clarisa. I think the thing to do is for you to go over there. See if you can get anything else out of Clarisa. Talk to Aaron and see if you can get him to tell the truth about that night," Carson said.

"Alright, I'll head over there first thing next week," Matt said.

"No, please, go over there as soon as you can. I am under a lot of pressure here, Mr. Dawson. Everyday we fail to take the money out of this vicious woman's hands, is another day she has to squander it on some stupid rat hole."

"I know but..." Matt said.

"Please, Mr. Dawson, Martin Justin said his friend Frank assured him that you could be counted on," Carson said.

"Alright, I'll get over there by tomorrow," Matt said.

"Thanks, we are counting on you," Carson said and he hung up.

Quincey was glaring at him.

"You're running out on me?"

"Look, here's what I'll do. I'll drive over to Phoenix this afternoon, work the case for a couple of days and fly back here Saturday morning. We can go to the shindig, and I'll go back over there Sunday evening," Matt said.

"Alright. I'll pick up a tux for you. You promise you'll be here?"

"Scout's honor."

Twelve

Matt pulled out on Interstate 8 heading east to Arizona. He pushed his Z3 along, scooting around the slower traffic, quickly leaving the marine layer of San Diego and heading into the coastal mountain range and the desert beyond.

Six hours of driving with only one stop in Yuma for gas and he was on the freeway coming into the metropolitan area. It only occurred to him at that point that he had no idea where in the sixth largest city in the country that Clarisa could be found. Matt pulled out his cell phone and called Carson Ashton.

"Do you have an address for Clarisa now?" Matt asked when Carson came on the line.

"Just a minute."

A few minutes later he came back to the phone. "Yes, sorry, they live in Scottsdale, not Phoenix. It's to the east of Phoenix," Carson said.

"Could you give me the address?"

Matt pulled off the freeway and into a shopping center parking lot and wrote the address down in his notebook. He saw a Safeway in the shopping center so he drove over to it, went in and found a Phoenix area and a Scottsdale City map. The clerk noticed Matt studying the map and asked, "Can I help you find anything?"

"Yes, there seem to be more freeways here than I remember. I'm going to an address in north Scottsdale, what's the best way to get there?" Matt asked.

"Stay on 10 through the center of town and then get on the 202. Stays on it until it crosses 101, then go north. It goes up the eastern edge of Scottsdale."

Matt had been in Phoenix a few times before but the area had greatly changed. He noticed the Bank One Ballpark with its roof open. It was one of the first baseball parks to have a closeable roof. He was surprised to see a large lake next to the freeway before he got to the 101. Traffic was heavy until he got on the 101 north. He got off at the Shea Boulevard exit and went east a few blocks to 192nd street.

After driving north a few blocks in a dense residential area he drove by Woody

Montana's home. The place took up most of a city block. The entrance was marked

by a set of large brick walls each adorned with a large sculpture of a buffalo. The

long driveway led back to a circular drive in front of a large red roof tiled house. To

the north, most of the land was fenced in to form several large buffalo pens. Matt

counted eight or nine animals in the front pen. Some were standing out in the sun

but most huddled under a large shade cover. Matt drove slowly around the block.

More buffalo were in the pen on the far side of the lot. A large cattle trailer was

parked out in the far lot, with 'Woody Montana, the buffalo man,' emblazoned on its

side. Matt noted a plain colored sedan parked on the side of the street. It wouldn't

have been noticeable except that a woman was sitting in the front seat, slumping

down somewhat. Matt had been on too many stakeouts not to know that she was

sitting there waiting and watching the Woody Montana spread. Matt drove on past

and circled the block a second time. The sedan was still there. The driver looked

back at Matt as he drove slowly past. She didn't look too pleased. As he went up to

the next corner and turned, he saw the sedan pull out into the street and turn into a

driveway, backing up and driving off in the opposite direction. Matt stopped, turned

around and caught site of the sedan as it drove off to the south. Matt picked up the

sedan and followed at a distance. The sedan went west down Shea Boulevard,

moving in and out of traffic. At a traffic light near Scottsdale Road, the sedan turned

left and into a small hotel. As Matt pulled into the hotel entryway, he saw the

woman get out of the sedan. She had parked off to the side of the hotel.

"This is as good a place to stay as any," Matt said to himself and he pulled into

the driveway where the sign indicated parking for check in only.

Matt went into the lobby and was about to walk over to the check in counter

when the sedan lady came through the door at the back.

She saw Matt and glared at him, walked up and said, "Why are you following me?"

"Who me? I'm just going to check in."

"What's your interest in the buffalo ranch?" she said.

"What's yours?" Matt responded.

"Mexican standoff," she said.

"OK, I'll tell if you tell. Hi, my name is Matt Dawson."

"Peggy McClure."

"Tell you what, Peggy McClure. I'll check in and get my stuff up to a room and then meet you in the bar in half and hour and we can exchange confidences," Matt said.

Peggy smiled and said, "Alright."

"Great, see you in thirty minutes."

Matt checked in and put his gear in a room on the second floor in the back of the hotel. Matt washed his face, changed his shirt and headed down to the bar.

Matt entered the bar and glanced around. No sign of Peggy McClure. He found a seat at a booth in the back. The waitress came over and he ordered a drink. In a few minutes, Peggy entered the bar. She was an attractive auburn haired girl in her mid thirties. She probably had a good figure under those somewhat butch clothes. She had green eyes and a pretty smile. She had changed into a pair of jeans and a light colored pullover with a western vest. Matt wondered if she had on boots with all that. She stood at the bar entrance, her eyes adjusting to the light, and headed over to Matt's booth. Matt stood up and said 'Hi, thought maybe you weren't coming," as she sat down across from him.

"Wouldn't miss it," she said.

"What would you like to drink?"

"A glass of white zinfandel," she said as the waitress came over.

"You want to trade cards?" Matt asked.

"Sure."

Matt pulled out his from his wallet and Peggy reached into a fanny pack and pulled out one of hers. They both studied the cards for a minute.

"Shall I start? What does Global World Insurance want with Woody Montana?" Matt asked.

"Nothing. I'm following up on an insurance policy that was on Devin Ashton, the current Mrs. Montana's previous husband," Peggy said.

"Yes, I remember Detective Kerns mentioning that policy, it doesn't pay off if Ashton was murdered?"

"Right. Now my turn. What's your interest in Woody Montana?" Peggy said.

"My interest is more with Clarisa as well. Her stepson, Carson Ashton is suing her for control of the Ashton fortune. I've been cataloging all the accidents she has been associated with during her lifetime and the death of Devin Ashton in particular," Matt said.

"Sounds like we could be on the same team," Peggy said.

"What do you hope to find out by staking out the buffalo ranch?" Matt asked.

"I've been watching the Montanas for a few days, seeing how I might get closer to them, possibly pick up something useful. How about you? You're not very under cover in that sports car," she said.

"Wasn't going to go undercover. Clarisa knows that Carson Ashton has hired me. She says she wants to help in anyway she possibly can. I just rolled into town and decided to look over the place," Matt said.

"Have you talked with Detective Kerns?" Peggy said.

"Yes, a few days ago," Matt said.

"He thinks the maid did it," Peggy said.

"That's because there was no butler," Matt said.

"Right. I think this wasn't the first time Clarisa has killed someone," Peggy said.

"You think Clarisa killed Devin?" Matt asked.

"Yes, I read Kerns' report on how he had discovered that the car used in the killing. It had been parked down in San Mateo the night of the murder and rolled into the bay the next day or night off a nearby pier.   He timed the distances from the tennis club to the parking lot and back to the Ashton house in Pacific Heights," Peggy said.

"Really?"

"You didn't know all that?" Peggy asked.

"Did he say how he found out which car was used to kill Ashton?"

"No, I don't think he did," Peggy said.

"Well, I'm pretty certain you're right. Clarisa has probably killed five people at least in her career as an undercover serial killer," Matt said.

"Five?"

"Yes, you said she probably had killed someone. Who would that be?" Matt asked.

"I am certain she killed a man named Howard Peterson, a stock broker who lived in San Francisco," Peggy said.

"Yes, he is on my list of five," Matt said.

"I knew Howard. The police report says he had ingested heroin and a great deal of alcohol and that in some inebriated state. He drowned in his own bathtub. Howard hated the very idea of drugs and always drank moderately. He was with Clarisa when he died. I'm sure she drugged him and pushed him down in the water," Peggy said.

"The trouble with Clarisa is that she doesn't look the murderer part and never leaves any physical evidence of her misdeeds," Matt said.

"She was livid that Howard was not going to marry her. He had been taken with her looks but saw deeper into her character and didn't like what he saw," Peggy said.

"Sounds like you knew Howard pretty well," Matt said.

"Yes, I did."

Peggy didn't want to add anything more so Matt moved on.

"How about some dinner? I know a special Chinese restaurant that a friend recommended.   You can fill me in on what else you have learned about Clarisa," Matt said.

"OK, I'll put you on my expense account," Peggy said.

"Well, let's go Dutch. Come on, I'm hungry," Matt said.

"Let's take your Z3, I've never been in one of those," Peggy said.

They climbed into the Z3. Matt went back down to the 101 freeway and north a few miles to the Frank Loyld Wright exit. A few blocks east they found Flo's Unique Chinese Cuisine. The small restaurant was simply but attractively decorated in a new strip mall. The hotter items were printed in red on the menu.

"How did you know about this place?" Peggy asked after they had been seated.

"My friend and unofficial partner, Frank Pullen, used to fly into Phoenix and he started coming here," Matt said.

"Why did he fly here?" Peggy asked.

"He was an American Airlines pilot."

They ordered three items and agreed to share them.

"What else have you found out about Devin Ashton's murder?" Matt asked.

"Did you say you have Kern's report?"

"I had some input into it," Matt said.

"The woman that bought the car that was used to murder Ashton drove up to the dealership in a red Miata, which is what Maria drives," Peggy said.

"Yes, I know."

"So I asked Maria if she let Clarisa drive her car. She said she had never asked to, so I asked her where she kept her keys. She said they were on top of her

dresser most of the time. She only picked them up when she went out in the car,"
Peggy said.

"So Clarisa could have easily gotten to them," Matt said.

"Yes. Maria said that she and Aaron Ashton were over in Lake Tahoe the
weekend that the car was purchased. I went over there and talked to the caretaker
of a condo-unit across from where the Ashton's cottage is. He remembered Aaron
and his red Porsche. He said he had a pretty girl with him on that weekend," Peggy
said.

"I think we can rule out Maria. Did you tell Kerns about all this?" Matt asked.

"I sent him a report the other day. I haven't heard back from him," Peggy said.

"What do you expect to learn by being here in Arizona?" Matt asked.

"I usually work best undercover. If I get close to someone who has a secret they
often brag about it when they get to know you," Peggy said.

"Sneaky one, huh?" Matt said.

"Whatever works, as they say," Peggy said.

Their dinners came. The general feeling was that the food was excellent and in fact
unique as advertised. Peggy told Matt how she had become an insurance
investigator after a career in police work. She lived in San Francisco in a house in
the Marina District. She lived in the top floor with her cat and rented out the bottom
apartment.

"You're out of San Diego. How did you get a case in San Francisco?" Peggy
asked.

"The client had a feeling that Clarisa had made too big an impression on the San
Francisco establishment for them to even consider her as a suspect," Matt said.

"That's certainly proved true. It's taken a lot for Kerns to even agree to check
Clarisa out," Peggy said.

On the way back to the hotel Peggy asked, "So what's your approach to the problem?"

"Direct, Clarisa claims to want to be helpful, so I'm going to call her in the morning and see if I can drop by for a few questions," Matt said.

"Hmmm, I like sneaky better."

The next morning Matt called Clarisa and she seemed almost glad to hear from him.

"I wondered how you were coming in your investigation. I think I might have something to add at this point. Why don't you come by at ten? We'll be having brunch on the patio which I hope you would join us for," Clarisa said on the phone.

Matt agreed and drove up the driveway past the twin buffalo statues at two minutes to ten. He parked behind the red Porsche again and went up the stone walkway to the front door. A burly fellow in a western shirt and jeans answered the door.

"What'd ya want?"

"Matt Dawson, I have an appointment with Clarisa Ashton, er, Mrs. Montana," Matt said.

"Who is it Dirk?" someone asked from inside the house.

"It's a guy named Dawson," Dirk said back over his shoulder.

A second man also dressed in a western shirt and jeans came up to the door. He was a good looking man, tall and thin, about thirty-five with a thin smile.

"Howdy, I'm Woody Montana. This is Dirk Smith my ranch foreman. You must be the guy trying to find out what happened to Clarisa's previous husband."

"Yes sir, Matt Dawson, thank you for seeing me," Matt said.

"Hey, no problem. I know Clarisa is as anxious as anyone to find out who killed Mr. Ashton. Come on in. Clarisa said you would be joining us for snack this morning."

Matt followed Montana through the house out to the back patio. The patio was shaded with an ivy-covered lattice. The floor was large Mexican tile. A barbecue unit was off to one side with a beehive fireplace at the other end. A waterfall flowed into a small swimming pool. Clarisa had brought her horn-rimmed glasses with the gold chain from California and sat at a small table holding a cup of coffee. Montana walked over and leaned down and kissed his wife.

"Your detective is here, sugar," Montana said. He took a chair beside Clarisa.

Clarisa held out her hand out to Matt. "I was surprised to hear you'd followed me all the way over here to Arizona, but I'm glad to see you again. I think I can help with your investigation. Please sit down," Clarisa said.

"Thank you," Matt said and he pulled up a chair. He noticed Clarisa and Montana were holding hands.

"There's a buffet over there against the house with a few breakfast items. You must let Carlita make you one of her omelets," Clarisa said.

"Some coffee would be fine, thanks," Matt said.

"Mr. Dawson,..." Clarisa said.

"Matt."

"Yes, Matt, I have been thinking about the night Devin died. I'm quite sure now that I did call down to Maria to ask her to bring me another bottle of Merlot, but she didn't answer the intercom. I had to go down stairs myself to get another bottle," Clarisa said.

"Did you go to her room? Did you check to see if she was there?" Matt asked.

"Why yes, I went to her door and knocked but got no answer. I assumed that she was sleeping so I got the wine myself," Clarisa said.

"So you think Maria might have left the house that evening?" Matt said.

"Yes, it's entirely possible. Detective Kerns told me how someone had purchased the car that killed Devin over in Oakland. I don't know if you know this, but Maria had a reason to be upset with Devin," Clarisa said.

"Really?"

"I hate to bring up old wounds, but Devin and Maria had an affair. Devin came to his senses and broke it off. I had no idea Maria could be that upset about it. I kept her on. It's so hard to find good help. But I think she has repaid my kindness with this awful thing she has done," Clarisa said and she turned to Montana for support.

"There, there honey," Montana said.

Matt felt nauseous.

"Yes, well you said before that you thought Aaron was at home that night as well. Do you still think he was in the house that night now that you've had more time to think about it?" Matt asked.

"I didn't see him. You can ask him yourself, he's here in Arizona with me you know," Clarisa said.

"Is he here now?" Matt asked glancing over to the pool to check for any nude swimmers.

"No, he's out with my brother David. David Wilkes is my brother. He is here in town visiting this week from Wyoming. Aaron is showing David and his girl friend some of the Arizona tourist attractions," Clarisa said.

"Got some interesting things to see here. Have you been to Arizona before?" Montana asked.

"A few times," Matt said.

"Hey, honey, why don't we have this young fellow over to our little party Saturday night? We're all going up to the Hyatt. They have an outdoor patio and some real good music. You could talk to Aaron then," Montana said.

"Can you come?" Clarisa asked.

"Yes, thanks," Matt said. Matt thought "I'm probably older that this 'young feller'. This might be a chance to talk to several people around the case on a one-to-one basis."

Matt finished his coffee and thanked the Montana's for their hospitality. They walked Matt back to the door. Montana had his arm draped around Clarisa's shoulders and it seemed like every other word was "honey" or "doll". The twenty-year age difference didn't seem to mean anything to them.

"We'll be in the Grotto Bar around eight," Woody said.

"The Scottsdale Hyatt Regency?"

"Yep," said Woody.

It wasn't until Matt had opened his car door that he remembered Quincey and her Saturday night formal appearance.

"Dam."

He drove back to the hotel and went to his room. With great trepidation he called Quincey.

"Hi Quincey. How are you?" Matt asked.

"Fine. How's your investigation going?"

"Very good. But, I ran into a hitch," Matt said.

"Like what?"

"The suspects have asked me to go to a party. I may have an opportunity to talk to several key people at once after they have had a drink or two. You don't get a chance to do this that often. I'm sorry, but I can't make it back for the charity event," Matt said and closed his eyes.

"What! You promised you'd be here. You can talk to those people some other time. Matt, you said you'd be here."

"Quincey, you have to do some things for your career. I need to do this for mine. I'm so sorry, I'll make it up to you," Matt said.

There was a long silence.

"Matt, I need some one I can count on," Quincey said.

"Aw, Quincey, I'm sorry," Matt said.

"For me, this is it, I don't want to see you anymore," Quincey said.

"Quincey, please…"

Quincey had hung up on him.

Matt cursed and hung up the phone.

Thirteen

It was the next afternoon and Matt had spent most the rest of the day feeling

sorry for himself. He tried to call Quincey back but she wouldn't answer the phone.

Finally, after a swim in the pool didn't help, he decided to try to do something useful

to shake it off. He set up his computer and ran his Profiler program on the various

new people he had met in the case. He entered the names of Peggy McClure, Dirk

Smith and David Wilkes, Carlisa's brother. He had brought the little printer Frank

had purchased in Wyoming with him this time so he printed out the reports on the

new set of people. He was scanning the reports when his phone rang. It was Frank

returning his call.

"You blew town without telling me," Frank said.

"Yeah, Carson was upset and wanted me over here working the case immediately

or he was going to black ball me," Matt said.

"What's new?"

"Clarisa has sold the company, remarried and moved to Arizona," Matt said.

"She's moved fast, all this in just a few weeks," Frank said.

"Yeah, maybe she did some preplanning," Matt said.

"That could be. Laura and I are heading over there for our annual Biltmore visit.

We'll be over there Monday afternoon." Frank said.

"What, you have a plan to hit all the four star resorts?" Matt asked.

"Only the ones that are managed by a friend that will comp half the stay," Frank

said.

"You know the Biltmore Manager?"

"He was at another hotel in Baltimore when I flew in there regularly, got to be

good friends. Anyway, we are checking in there Monday evening, let's have dinner,"

Frank said.

"OK, I'll call up to your room Monday about six thirty. Will that give you enough

time? Matt asked.

"We'll be there," Frank said and he rang off.

Getting back to his Profiler reports, Matt noticed that Dirk Smith had a prison record.

He had been put away for armed robbery. David Wilkes had tried an unsuccessful

initial public offering of stock for his retail operation. Peggy McClure checked out as

a former police officer and current insurance investigator.

Matt whiled away the rest of the day reading over the other Profiler reports about

people in the case. He put in a call to Detective Kerns but he was off duty. At seven

thirty he headed out for the Hyatt Regency Scottsdale. It was only a few blocks from

his hotel in distance but miles away in luxury level. He drove up the palm-lined

driveway and gave his keys to the parking valet. The large entry was an imposing

marble structure. Matt picked up a pamphlet about the resort as he went through the

lobby. The Hyatt boasted a golf course, ten swimming pools, a three-story water

slide, and a lagoon with a sand beach. The lobby opened up to a beautifully lighted

patio with a tall Saguaro cactus in the center of the area. Several of the swimming

pools were at the other end of the patio nestled among hundreds of tall palm trees.

A bar was off to the right of the area and a couple of dozen tables with rattan-

cushioned chairs around them. Matt spotted the Montanas and their entourage at a

table close to the bar. Woody got up as Matt approached.

"Hey, pardoner, glad you could make it," Woody said getting up and shaking

Matt's hand.

"This is a beautiful hotel," Matt said.

"It's something, ain't it? Honey, Matt is here," Woody said turning to Clarisa.

"Hello, Matt. How are you tonight?" Clarisa said.

"Fine, thanks," Matt said.

"Let me get you something to drink. What will you have?" Woody asked.

"Some white wine would go nicely."

Carlisa leaned back in her chair. "Matt, I want you to meet my new golfing friend. We played a round this morning and she's a great golfer."

The young woman turned around from her conversation with the man on her right. It was Peggy McClure.

"Matt Dawson." He extended his hand.

"Hi, I'm Peggy McClure."

"Nice to meet you," Matt said with a smile.

The band started up with a soft jazz rendering.

"Why don't you two get the dancing started," Woody said.

"My pleasure. Care to dance?" Matt asked Peggy.

Matt and Peggy and several other couples moved out to the dance floor.

"Funny meeting you here," Matt said.

"And you as well," Peggy said.

"How did you manage to get to play golf with Clarisa?"

"Just sneaky stuff. One of her regulars is a real estate sales person. I put in a call to her office that I was really interested in one of her properties, but I could only come by on the morning of her tee time with Clarisa. I was standing there when this message came through and her friend said she couldn't play. Simple," Peggy said.

"You are sneaky. Found anything out yet?" Matt asked

"Only that Clarisa has a nasty temper when she misses a shot," Peggy said.

"Who doesn't? Who's the guy you were talking to?" Matt asked.

"That's Clarisa's brother, David Wilkes. He thinks a lot of himself. Going to be the next great business success story, he tells me."

"Who else is at the table?" Matt asked.

"Let's see, Woody, Clairsa, David, her brother and a woman that's with David, I didn't catch her name. Aaron is over at the bar trying to hit on some chick. Oh, and that bodyguard or whatever he is, Dirk Smith, is around somewhere," Peggy said.

"Dirk Smith is the head buffalo wrangler. All these rich folks and us two gumshoes, a dandy group it is," Matt said.

The music ended.

"Yeah, we better get to work," Peggy said.

Woody had put Matt's drink in front of the chair off to Clarisa's left. Next to him was Aaron, returning from the bar. Matt recognized Jenny Paladora sitting next to Aaron. He went over to her.

"Ms. Paladora, Matt Dawson, we met in your office in Cheyenne," Matt said.

"Hello, again. Surprised to see you here in Arizona," Jenny said.

"I'm following up on Devin Ashton's case. How are you enjoying your visit?" Matt asked.

"Fine. I hadn't been here in a long time. Have you met David?" Jenny asked.

"No, I don't believe I have," Matt said.

Jenny turned to David Wilkes, "David, this is Matt Davidson."

"Matt Dawson," Matt said and he extended his hand to Wilkes.

"Nice to meet you Mr. Dawson, you live here?" Wilkes asked.

"No, I'm from out of town as well. I live in San Diego," Matt said.

"Really, I have some good contacts over there. Do you know Charelton Kendel? He runs a chain of fast food restaurants. Growing like crazy," Wilkes said.

"No, sorry," Matt said.

Matt sat down and sipped his drink.

"So how is Carson taking my little changes in lifestyle?" Clarisa asked Matt.

"He's a little upset," Matt said. Understatement was his forte.

"Well, if he would be reasonable I might change things. Aaron has understood my need to start anew. He's such a fine young man," Clarisa said.

"The Children's Cancer Hospital was counting on support," Matt reported.

"It's a fine organization in its own way, but I think there may be other, more deserving causes. I have always felt a certain kinship with the Native Americans you know. It's my responsibility now to see that Devin's money is used wisely. I feel I must make my own choices," Clarisa said.

"You have made a lot of changes very rapidly," Matt said.

"Yes, it's a miracle, to find someone you really care for, a second time in life," Clarisa said.

"You've been married three times, haven't you Mrs. Ashton?" Matt asked.

"I keep forgetting you're a detective. Yes, but the first one doesn't count. I was so young and foolish," Clarisa said.

"It was love at first sight?" Matt asked.

"Yes, I think Woody liked me for who I am, not the money. I didn't even have him sign a pre-nuptial," Clarisa said.

No need if you are simply going to get rid of him when he not useful anymore Matt thought to himself.

The band started another danceable number and Woody and Clarisa got up as well as Jenny and David Wilkes. Peggy headed out to the powder room leaving Matt and Aaron alone at the table.

"Aaron, I'm glad I have this opportunity to talk to you," Matt said.

"Really, why?" Aaron said. He showed the affects of several drinks.

"The police are tending toward arresting Maria for your father's death," Matt said.

"That's ridiculous," Aaron said.

"If they do, they may charge you with aiding and abetting the crime," Matt said.

Aaron put down his drink. Matt had his attention now.

"I didn't do anything. I would never have had my father killed," Aaron said.

"Do you know that Clarisa is now telling the police that she tried to talk to Maria on that night but she couldn't find her?" Matt asked.

"What?"

"I think it would be best if you told the police yourself what actually happened that night at the house. If you can give me some assurance it won't leave your hands, I'll let you see a copy of my report that I sent Carson. There may be a few things about Clarisa in it that you don't know," Matt said.

"OK, I promise to not let anyone else see it," Aaron said.

"Particularly not Clarisa?"

"Yes, alright. I take it you think Clarisa had something to do with my father's death?" Aaron asked.

"I'd put it a little stronger, but yes that's why I'm here. Again, read the report and make up your own mind. Meet me tomorrow at my hotel at noon and I'll show it to you," Matt said. He gave Aaron one of his cards with the hotel name and his room number on it.

The dance was over and everyone came back to the table.

"I need a smoke. Got to go out to the damn parking lot for a simple little cigarette," Woody said.

Matt didn't smoke but he said, "I'll go with you."

"Great, hate to go out there alone," Woody said.

As he followed Woody out he wondered what he was going to do with a cigarette. They moved off to one side of the hotel entrance and Woody pulled out a pack and offered Matt one. He took it and held it like he knew what he was doing. Woody lit his and offered a light to Matt.

It was the moment of truth. He sucked in and tried not to cough too much.

The thing was lit. He held it down to his side, avoiding the smoke as much as possible.

"You're a lucky man, Mr. Montana," Matt said.

"You mean Clarisa's money. You know we both just sort of clicked. Nobody believes me, but I didn't know she had money when I asked her to marry me," Woody said.

"Really?" Add another one to the list Matt thought.

"No, really I didn't. I knew she was married, but not happy. Then her husband got killed. I may have taken advantage of her situation, being left all alone and all. But I really love her. As far as the money goes, when we were talking about getting hitched, she said something about no pre-nuptial agreement. I thought she was thinking about a pre-nuptial so that I could protect my daughter. What little I have that will be hers someday. My little buffalo ranch is worth quite a bit, you know. I was married once myself. Have a daughter up in Denver," Woody said.

"You never saw her house or found out who Devin Ashton was?" Matt asked.

"Not really. Someone said he was into ventures or something. I had no idea that he was filthy rich. Clarisa usually drove herself over to my hotel when we got together so I never went to her house. After we were married I did go over there once. I wasn't too impressed. It's a real old house on a little bity lot, no acreage to speak of," Woody said.

"Probably worth several million," Matt said.

"Oh that California real estate is crazy," Woody said.

"The money is half yours now," Matt said.

"Yeah, my god, there's enough to pave a gold brick highway through town," Woody said.

"Something like two hundred million, I understand," Matt said.

"I haven't tried to spend any of it. Well, I did buy one toy. I got me a new boat," Woody said.

"Oh, I love boats myself, what kind?" Matt asked.

"It's a twenty eight foot Chriscraft cabin cruiser with a three twenty eight engine. It's a beaut," Woody said.

"Where have you got it?"

"It's going to be out on a lake north of here. It's a big one, Lake Pleasant. What kind of boat have you got?" Woody asked.

"It's a sailboat. I have it at a marina on San Diego Bay. I live on it," Matt said.

"A sailboat guy, huh? Always preferred something with an engine myself. Feel like I need to have some power when I put out on the water. Say, watch your finger," Woody said.

Matt's cigarette was about to burn his finger. He flicked off the ash and stomped it out.

"You don't smoke, do you?" Woody asked.

"Yeah, I wanted to get some air," Matt said.

Woody quietly said, "Clarisa thinks her maid is the one that killed Ashton."

"Yes, she mentioned that," Matt said.

"Can't imagine what was going through Ashton's mind when he fooled around on Clarisa," Woody said.

"The age difference between you two doesn't bother you?" Matt asked.

"Naw, I have had my share of pretty little things with no mind beyond getting to the next shopping spree. Clarisa is a fun, sexy woman and a real partner for me," Woody said.

The band started up another number. Woody put out his cigarette.

"Let's get back to the party," he said.

Matt took turns dancing with Clarisa, Peggy and Jenny Paladora. Clarisa was the best dancer. While she was alone with Matt she said again how sad she felt that Maria had been so hurt as to cause her to be a murderer. At about one am they all decided to call it a night. Matt offered to take Peggy back to the hotel.

When they were in the Z3 and headed back, Matt asked, "Well, did you pick up anything new?"

"Only that David Wilkes is in Clarisa's new will, and that Clarisa has them all convinced that Maria the maid killed Devin Ashton. What did you learn?" Peggy asked.

"Woody had no idea that Clarisa was filthy rich when he married her," Matt said.

"Right," Peggy said.

Fourteen

On Sunday Matt slept in late. After breakfast he tried calling Quincey again but she had all her calls go through her answering machine. She wasn't picking up.

At noon, Aaron came into the hotel restaurant and sat down with Matt. Matt ate his sandwich while Aaron read through the report. When he put down the document he looked somewhat stunned.

"How much of this are you certain of?" Aaron asked.

"I'm reasonably certain of all of it," Matt said.

"I'm pretty sure I heard Clarisa's car leave the house that night," Aaron said.

"Why didn't you tell this before now?"

"I just heard a car. I never thought that it might have been Clarisa."

"Will you tell the police this?" Matt asked.

"I need to think about this. I can't know for sure it was Clarisa," Aaron said.

"Remember, Clarisa has no problems implicating Maria, and that means you as well," Matt said.

"I'll get back to you," Aaron said and got up and left.

Matt finished his lunch and went upstairs. He tried Quincey again. There was no answer. He put on his bathing suit. Out by the pool he found Peggy taking in a few rays. He sat down beside her.

"How are you feeling today," Peggy asked.

"Fine, how about you?" Matt said.

"You looked down. Hangover?" Peggy asked.

Matt laughed, "No, woman trouble."

"Oh, how's that?"

"My girlfriend sent me packing. She won't even talk to me. I promised her I'd take her to a fancy party last night. Instead, I spent it dancing with a murderer," Matt said.

"It's hard to do this type of job and have any type of relationship," Peggy said.

"Do you have a boy friend or something?" Matt asked.

"What do you mean, 'something'?" Peggy asked.

"You could be married," Matt said.

"No wedding ring here. I can't keep a husband or boy friend either," Peggy said.

"You were married?" Matt asked.

"Just once," Peggy said.

"I think I wasted an evening. We didn't learn much."

"You can never tell what is going to be useful, but, you're right. I'm thinking I'll get back to San Francisco after the little boat trip," Peggy said.

"What boat trip?" Matt asked.

"Clarisa asked me to go with them on their boating and overnight camping trip up to Lake Pleasant. They are breaking in their new cabin cruiser," Peggy said.

"Well, you're really in with them," Matt said.

Matt cell phone rang. It was Woody Montana.

"Say, Matt, how are you today?" Woody said.

"Fine, just sitting here by the pool."

"Listen, Tuesday we are taking the new boat out for camping trip up to that lake I was telling you about. It's an overnighter. We'll have a campfire, cook some buffalo steaks. How about coming along?"

"Sure, I'd like to," Matt said.

"I remember you said you like to sail, so I'll have a sailboat waiting for you at the dock. We'll have a race," Woody said.

"That would be great. I've heard the lakes here are good for sailing. I think I'll put my money on you as far as the race goes," Matt said.

"Meet us at the Lake Pleasant Marina at about ten Tuesday morning," Woody said.

Matt hung up. "I guess I'm in too. Woody is putting a sailboat at my disposal."

"I'd say you are winning the 'whose in' contest."

After a minute she said, "Familiarity breeds contempt, but what if you already have contempt?"

"Somehow I feel like this is personal with you," Matt said.

Peggy put on her sunglasses. "What are you going to do this afternoon?" she asked.

"No plans."

"How about I take you to a movie," she said.

"Alright, sounds good."

They each returned to their rooms, met again, and took in a movie. After the show Matt took Peggy for dinner.

The next day, Monday, Matt tried calling Quincey at her office. Her secretary would take the message but she said Quincey was too busy to come to the phone. He had better luck getting through to detective Kerns.

"Haven't got the results back from the lab on those fingerprints. It took me a while to get a set of Clarisa's prints. Carson Ashton helped me with that," Kerns said.

"You know that Clarisa is now living here in Arizona?" Matt said.

"Yes, Carson told me about that. You're there now?"

"I've met her new husband. He might be next on her list," Matt said.

Kerns laughed. "Could be. I'm still keeping an open mind about Maria the maid."

Matt concluded his call to Kerns, promising to stay in touch about Clarisa's movements. Kerns said he would call as soon as he had the results of the fingerprint checks.

Matt called Carson Ashton.

"Have you been able to talk to Clarisa?" Carson asked.

"Yes, she has been most approachable. She is pitching the story to anyone that will listen that Maria is the killer," Matt said.

"Did you talk to Aaron?"

"Yes, I showed him the report on Clarisa I had given you. I think he may have had his eyes opened," Matt said.

"Will he testify?"

"He's thinking about it. I think Clarisa might cut a deal on the money," Matt said.

"I'll bet she would. That would be better than having us keep the pressure on to discover her murdering ways," Carson said.

"I'm going on a boating-camping trip with them tomorrow. Then I think I'll head back. I don't see what else I can do here," Matt said.

"Maybe it would be better to concentrate on the details of what went on the night my father was killed," Carson said.

Around six o'clock Matt headed over to the Arizona Biltmore. This hotel was one of the two of the four-star resorts in Arizona. Matt remembered the myth that Frank Lloyd Wright had designed it in the late 1920's. Its gray earth tone building materials were famous architecturally. At one point Matt had considered becoming an architect himself. Actually Wright served as a consultant, assisting his former student, Albert McArthur. The Biltmore is the grand dame of the Arizona tourist industry.

Matt called Frank's room from the lobby. Laura answered.

"Laura, it's Matt. Are you ready to go eat?" Matt asked.

"Frank is running late as usual and you are right on time as usual. I'll hurry him up. See you in the lobby in about ten minutes," Laura said.

Matt strolled the lobby and looked at a map showing the layouts of the two golf courses surrounding the hotel. Matt had once tried to play golf but had given it up in favor of tennis. The hotel also had a fine group of tennis courts.

Frank and Laura came out of the elevator.

"Hi, Matt," Laura said and gave him a big hug. Laura looked trim and fit in her little black number. A touch of jewelry set her eyes off.

"Are you keeping busy here in the Grand Canyon State?" she asked.

"Somewhat busy but I'm not sure about effective. How was your trip?" Matt said.

"Oh, great. We always get an audiotape to listen to on the way over. It really helps the time go by," Laura said.

"Shall we eat here? I made some reservations," Frank said.

"Sure," Matt said.

When they had been seated at the table with a view out to the pool, Frank asked, "So, how is it going? Is your trip over here getting you any closer to proving what Clarisa has done?"

"I may have Aaron on the verge of telling what he knows about the night Ashton was killed. He heard a car leave. I showed him the report I had sent Carson. It may have changed his mind about Clarisa," Matt said.

"Any word from the Frisco police?" Frank said.

"They are still checking the finger prints found at the pier."

The waiter came and Matt and Laura ordered lobster and Frank had salmon.

"You realize we have come to the desert and ordered fish," Frank said.

"What do you hear from Quincey?" Laura asked.

"Nothing, nothing at all. She says she doesn't want to ever see me again," Matt said.

"Oh, I'm sorry to hear that. What happened?" Laura asked.

"Maybe he doesn't want to talk about it," Frank interjected.

"It's ok. She's right. I'm away too much. She needs someone that can accompany her to her functions. I thought I could get back for that charity ball last Saturday, but I had a chance to get together with Clarisa and her latest set of associates. Looking back I wish I would have gone back like Quincey wanted me to," Matt said.

"Did you learn anything?" Frank asked.

"I got a chance to talk to Aaron alone, as I mentioned, but other than that, not much. I am going on a boating outing tomorrow with them," Matt said.

"You might not have been invited to that if you had skipped getting together Saturday night," Frank said.

"I know how much Quincey was counting on going to that ball. She bought a special dress. Matt, you shouldn't make promises unless you are going to keep them," Laura said.

"You got me there."

Matt fell silent and Laura starting recalling a trip she had made down into the Grand Canyon on mule back. Frank said that he would rather fly around it than get saddle sore.

Matt was thinking about his misfortune of losing women that he cared for. First his wife that had died in childbirth. He still carried a wound from that. Then another one, a client that died in his arms. Now, Quincey had told him to get lost. Maybe, she wasn't for him. She traveled in a higher velocity plane. She liked being a minor celebrity. He suddenly realized that Laura was talking to him.

"Sorry, what?" Matt asked.

"How much longer are you going to stay here?" Laura asked.

"I think I'll head back after this little outing," Matt said.

"It's somewhat surprising that Carlisa wants to socialize with you. She knows you are working for Carson and he is trying to sue to get control of the money," Frank said.

Matt took a sip of water. "I think maybe she wants a way to communicate with Carson through me and she also wants to know where we are in the investigation."

"What makes you think that?" Frank asked.

"She said she might make a deal on the money in so many words."

"Well, it should be interesting for you," Frank said.

"At least I get to do some desert sailing."

Fifteen

The next morning Peggy and Matt set out for the lake in Matt's dark blue Z3. Peggy had called over and mentioned to Clarisa that she would be going to the lake with Matt.

"You two must have hit it off. I must warn you though, Matt is a detective. He's trying to find out who the hit and run driver was that killed my last husband," Clarisa said.

"Really. I'll be careful of what I say," Peggy said.

"No need. I want to find this person just as much as anyone else," Clarisa said.

Matt took the new freeway system over to the Black Canyon Freeway and headed north. They passed a couple of hills, strewn with black volcanic rocks that gave the road its name and then went past a large prison.

"Maybe there's a cell in there with Clarisa's name on it. If we finally get something concrete on Clarisa, I guess they will have to extradite her," Peggy said.

"That would generate a great deal of lawyer income for sure," Matt said.

"With her money, she can probably beat that and never have to pay for what she has done," Peggy said.

"Usually things that you do wrong have a way of coming back to get you," Matt said.

They came to the turnoff for Lake Pleasant and headed out west of the main freeway. Phoenix was built on a flat valley plain made by the Salt River and ringed by desert mountains. On the drive to the lake they left the valley behind and entered more dramatic terrain. Another smaller river, the Auga Fria, had been dammed up creating one of the first efforts in the desert west to provide a reliable water source. In more recent times Arizona had made use of its share of the Colorado River water when the Central Arizona Project was built. The CAP carries water from Lake Havasu near Parker all the way to the Indian reservation southwest of Tucson. Lake Pleasant is the main storage facilities for the CAP. The new Waddell

Dam kept the name of the original but greatly expanded the size of the lake.

Matt pulled into the entrance to the Lake Pleasant Marina, a bright new facility

with a gated entrance. It was after ten AM when he drove through the main parking

lot and spotted the Montana party.

Aaron, Woody and Dirk Smith were studying a map laid out on the hood of the

cream colored Lexus RX400 sports utility. The doors of the car were open and

Clarisa and Jenny Paladora were sitting in the back seat. David Wilkes was off to the

side taking some pictures of the marina. Another young woman in a bikini stood

behind the map conference with her hands on her hips. Matt pulled up beside the

group. Peggy and Matt got out of the Z3.

"Good morning. Ready to face nature?" Woody asked.

"Sure. You need a map for that?" Matt asked.

"Dirk here was showing us where he has set up the camp. He came in earlier

and took a load of stuff up there in a run about," Woody said.

Evidently this was a full-scale invasion of the outdoors. Parked beside the SUV

was a pickup chock full of camping gear.

Woody indicated a spot on the map. "Look here, Matt. We're set up here, in this

cove, around this point. Think you can get a sailboat all the way up there?"

"I reckon," Matt said.

Clarisa and Jenny Paladora got out of the SUV.

"Let's get on with it, Woody. I'm getting bored and hot just sitting in the car,"

Clarisa said.

"Give us a minute, Honey, to get organized," Woody said.

Aaron turned to Matt. "Hi, this is Melody. I met her the other night at the hotel."

"Hi, Melody, I'm Matt and this is Peggy," Matt said to the bikini.

Melody hied back.

Matt and Peggy had on baseball caps, t-shirts and shorts. Clarisa had on something that would have been suitable for an African Safari. Woody, Aaron and Dirk all had on cowboy hats, blue jeans and cowboy shirts. David Wilkes seemed the least suitable in his dress slacks and a polo sports shirt. Jenny Paladora was in shorts and was sporting a western hat.

"Dirk will show you where the sailboat is, Matt. We'll put some of the gear aboard that and the rest on my boat. Peggy, you want to go up there with Matt on his slow boat or come with us on my new toy?" Woody asked.

"Oh, I'll keep Matt company," Peggy said.

"Matt, come on out to the dock and see my new boat. Dirk will take you over to the sailboat I rented for you. Alright, everybody pick something out of the truck and let's get the rest of this stuff out to the boat," Woody said.

Everyone but Clarisa and David picked up parts of the camping gear from the back of the pickup and they started the trek down to the docks where the new boat was tied up.

The bright shiny new twenty-eight foot Christcraft suitably impressed Matt. The front cabin easily soaked up all the gear they had brought down.

"Nice boat," Matt told Woody.

"Ain't she a beaut," Woody said.

"Where's the sail?" Matt asked.

"Ah now, we'll see who gets up the lake first," Woody said laughing.

"We'll head on up to the campsite, dump all this stuff so Dirk can set it up and then cruise the lake. I have water skis and fishing gear if you're interested," Woody said.

Matt and Peggy followed Dirk out and over to another dock where a twenty-five foot Catalina was tied up. Dirk could get the pickup closer to this location so he brought out the rest of the camping gear. He and Matt stored it in the sloop's cabin.

"You all set. Know how to get this rig going?" Dirk asked Matt.

"I think I can handle it," Matt said.

"Good, because I ain't got no idea. Meet you up at the campsite," Dirk said.

He moved down the dock to a run about with a small motor.

Matt started the sailboat's outboard motor. He had Peggy untie the bowline and they were off, moving out through the floating docks to the entrance of the little marina harbor area. Even though this was a weekday morning, several boats were moving about. The dam stretched off to their left as they left the harbor entrance. Matt turned the boat north and put the engine to full speed moving the boat smartly. A racing boat roared by, spewing out almost as much noise as a jet engine. Matt killed the outboard.

"What do we do now, row?" Peggy asked.

"Bend on the sails, lass, bend on the sails. Come over here and hold the boat into the wind," Matt said.

"What wind?"

"There's a light breeze," Matt said as Peggy took the tiller.

"How do I know where the wind is coming from?" Peggy asked.

"Look at the tell tale," Matt said.

"The what?"

"See this red thing up on the sail."

"Oh."

Matt found the main halyard and easily raised the main sail and then the jib. He went back and took the tiller from Peggy and a few minutes they were moving down the lake.

"Do you know how to sail?" Matt asked.

"No. Always been on power boats," Peggy said.

"If you want to learn I could show you how," Matt said.

"OK. That would be fun," Peggy said.

They had gone on another hundred yards or so when Matt saw the new Montana cabin cruiser coming up majestically behind them. Aaron and the bikini were sitting up on the bow. Clarisa and Jenny were sitting in the back under the awning while Woody and David sat in the captain's chairs amidships, driving the boat. The boat was moving relatively slowly but generating a large wake. Woody waved as they steamed past.

"There goes the cruise ship," Matt said as he waved back.

"You think they're on to me, sticking me out here with you?" Peggy said.

"No idea, but I'm not complaining," Matt said.

The bow wave from the powerboat made the sails flair and the sailboat lost speed and then picked it up again as Matt turned away from the wind to fill the sails.

"Don't we need to go that way?" Peggy said.

"With a sailboat you have to plot a way to get where you want to go depending on the wind. It's not usually a straight line. That's why it's more fun. Any dummy can point a boat at another point and drive over to it. With a sailboat it takes some skill to get where you want to go," Matt said.

"Hmmm."

Matt easily found the camp ground Woody had selected near the far end of the lake, on its eastern shore. He expertly rounded the point and pulled into the small cove. The Catalina 250 had a retractable keel which Matt brought up and the nosed the boat gently into the shore. Woody had already unloaded the camping gear and taken Aaron and his date water skiing. Dirk Smith had a Latin helper setting up the camp. It already looked like a village, with four tents, and two shade canopies. Dirk came up to the sailboat and helped Peggy off the side.

"Finally made it, huh?" Dirk said.

"Yes, we took the scenic route," Matt said.

"Could ya throw down the gear you got on board?" Dirk asked.

Matt pulled out the gear from the cabin and handed it out to Dirk.

"Looks like you're building a whole town," Matt said.

"Yeah, it's good that I have Juan helping me. Carlita is up there too. She can fix you some lunch," Dirk said.

Matt and Peggy walked up the little incline to the campsite and found Carlita hovering over a table set with various lunch items. She smiled and bowed her way off to the side while Matt and Peggy got plates and picked up a few items for lunch. Dirk and Juan were off to one end of the circle, putting in the last pegs to keep that tent up. David Wilkes sat under the other sun screen canopy in a lounge chair with a pair of binoculars staring out to the far shore. Clarisa came out of the tent on the far right of the circle.

"Well, you two finally made it," Clarisa said.

"Yes, I really enjoyed the sail, Mrs. Montana. I want to thank you for setting it up," Matt said.

"Oh, it was Woody's idea. He loves to please people, and usually me in particular. So I certainly don't mind," Clarisa said.

At that point the Chriscraft came roaring around the point and circled the point pulling the bikini on her water skis. Woody was at the wheel while Aaron watched the skier.

"We've set up four tents as you can see. Woody and I have this one, David and Jenny, Aaron and his friend. I thought you two could share the one on the other end. Each tent has two cots. Is that alright?" Clarisa said.

"No objections here," Peggy said.

"Nor me," Matt said.

Jenny Paladora came out of her tent. "Clarisa, could you help me get this bedroll straightened out? It's all tangled."

"Oh, this is like Girl Scout Camp," Clarisa said and she went to help.

"Maybe I can help too," Peggy said and she followed Clarisa.

Matt strolled over to a chair set up beside David Wilkes.

"What are you looking at?" Matt asked.

"Little Bald Eagles learning to feed. See there, there's one diving now," David said.

Matt shaded his eyes and watched the eaglet attempt to get a fish down in the shallows across the little cove.

"I understand that during part of the year they won't let anyone up here so that it won't interfere with this," David said.

Matt noticed that David was wearing a hairpiece that was off to one side and perspiration was dripping down the side of his head.

"Are you hot?" Matt asked.

"Yes. I probably should take my hair off. I'll do that anyway if I go swimming. I really don't like Jenny to see me without it," David said.

"Some women think bald is beautiful," Matt said.

The three women came over carrying drinks and pulled up camp chairs. Peggy brought Matt a glass of iced tea.

"It's so nice here, out in the open," Clarisa said.

Matt noticed that the wind had freshened.

"The wind is up. I think I'll take the boat out. You want to come?" Matt asked Peggy.

She agreed and they went down to the shore and pushed the boat back out into the cove. The breeze quickly caught the sails and Matt moved the boat out into the lake. The wind was now making waves with little white tops and the boat moved smartly. Matt let Peggy take the helm and showed her how you could put the boat into the various points of sail. They sailed back and forth across the lake numerous times, watching as Woody first pulled Jenny Paladora and then Aaron around on skis. Even David Wilkes managed to get up. David made a spectacular wipeout as they came in close behind Matt and Peggy. Several times Woody ran rings around the Catalina 250, laughing at the effect that the motor boat's bow wave had on the sailboat. Clarisa sat on the other captain's chair, with her safari hat secured with a scarf. At one point the motor boat stopped dead in the water. Matt and Peggy sailed by giving a grand wave to the group as Woody bent over the motor, making some adjustment. After another hour Woody took the motor boat in first while Matt and Peggy stayed out, enjoying the start of the evening breezes that flowed from the shore in the late afternoon. Finally the sun set. By the time they finally returned to the cove Dirk had a grill over the fire and was preparing for some serious cooking. Dirk and Juan had set up a camping table under one of the sun screen canopies. It boasted a white table cloth and fancy camp dinnerware. Somehow, Dirk had set up a large water dispenser between the two middle tents. Matt drew a bowl full and he and Peggy freshened up while Dirk and Carlita began cooking. The stars began coming out and soon they smell of roasting meat filled the air. All the campers gathered at the dinner table bathed in tiki torchlight. David had clearly gotten sunburned and everyone was hungry.

Only the bikini had changed. She had on a different bikini and a see through top. David had on his hair. Clarisa and Woody sat at opposite ends of the table while Matt, Peggy and the bikini sat opposite David, Jenny and Aaron. Carlita came around to each guest offering either red or white wine.

David offered a toast, "Here's to Woody's new boat, may she always ride the waves in style."

Aaron said, "Hear, hear. Let's eat already."

"We have either New York cuts, mahi-mahi or Buffalo steaks from the grill. Just let Carlita know which you would like," Woody said.

"Buffalo, huh?" Peggy said.

"Sure, Bison meat tastes great. It's real flavorful and tender. You cook it like regular steak," Woody said.

"I'll try the buffalo," Matt said. He noticed both of the people from Wyoming opted for meat from Kansas City.

A great silence followed after Carlita and Dirk served the food as everyone enjoyed the meal. The wine flowed freely.

"So, how do you like the buffalo, Matt?" Woody asked.

"It's good. Quite lean and tender. I like the taste," Matt said.

"See there, Aaron. You should try it," Woody said. Aaron had opted for the fish.

"Clarisa likes buffalo. When she was a kid she lived out on the reservation for a while you know," David said.

"Yes, it was part of a church program I was in one summer. We were supposed to get to know our fellow man and all. It was quite memorable," Clarisa said.

"What did you do while you were there? I don't remember this," Jenny asked.

"I think you were off to one of those student government things," Clarisa said.

"Oh, yes, I went to Denver with Bobby Bennington," Jenny said.

"She was real close to one family, tell them honey," Woody said.

"Yes, I spent a lot of time with one of the chief's family. I was about the same age as his youngest daughter. We had many meals together and we went to a pow-wow. They are simple, but noble people," Clarisa said.

"You were impressed?" Peggy said.

"The Sioux Indians have a creed they live by. They live simply, not wanting much. When the buffalo ran, they would only take enough to satisfy their everyday needs, usually just one buffalo a season for each family. In a way, it's the way I've tried to live my life. Take only what I need. No more and only when I need it. I've been lucky, of course. The men in my life have provided amply," Clarisa said.

Peggy seemed to be choking on a bite and Matt patted her on the back.

"You alright?" Matt said.

Peggy drank a sip of water. "Yes, I'm fine."

"You have had your share, haven't you," David said.

Clarisa gave David a steely glance.

"You've had your share, too, brother," she said.

"Yeah, and I helped you at a critical time to put you on the trail of that big buffalo herd out west," David said with a snear.

"And I helped you out with that last stock offering," Clarisa said.

"I told you that was just the initial phase," David said angrily.

"Let's not discuss this here," Clarisa said.

After a pause, several people at the table wondered what they were talking about.

"You're awfully quiet, Aaron. Was the fish alright?" Woody asked.

"Yes, fine. I was just remembering the first time I had mahi-mahi. It was in Hawaii, on the island of Kaui, on the trip when my mother was killed. Do you remember that Clarisa? You were with her when she died, weren't you?" Aaron said.

"It was an accident, Aaron," Clarisa said quietly.

"Oh, yes, that's what they told me," Aaron said and he look again down at his plate.

"Everybody done? How about some desert? We've got some fried ice cream," Woody said.

"Dirk can do that on the grill?" David asked.

"Well, I think Carlita is the one do'in it but it'll taste real good," Woody said.

"I always have that on my camping trips," Jenny said.

The deserts were good even if the ice cream was soft.

When they were done they moved over and spread out around the campfire while Dirk, Carlita and Juan cleared the dinner.

"That was an excellent meal, Woody," David said.

"Yes, thank you very much," Matt, Peggy, and Jenny echoed.

Aaron and his date had decided on a stroll along the lakeshore.

Woody got up and returned to the circle with an ice bucket carrying a champagne bottle.

"This'll keep the party going," Woody said.

Carlita brought each person a champagne glass and Woody did the honors.

"Are Carlita and Dirk and his helper staying out here with us?" Peggy asked.

"No, they'll take the little row boat back when they've finished cleaning up," Clarisa said.

"They'll be back in the morning to fix breakfast though," Woody said.

Everyone sipped their champagne and looked into the fire for a while. Aaron and the bikini came back and silently went over to their tent.

Dirk came over to Woody. "We're all done now. Guess we'll head on back."

"OK. Thanks Dirk, for a great meal," Woody said.

Everyone murmured agreement.

Juan, Clarlita and Dirk got in the run about, and Dirk started up the outboard. They went off into the night.

Woody threw some more wood on the fire. There was some talk about telling ghost stories but no one could remember one.

Woody got up and brought back another bottle of champagne. Everyone seemed thirsty. When that bottle was finally empty, Clarisa was feeling the wine.

"Yes sir, I got me some buffalo in my time," she said.

"Maybe you've had enough, honey," Woody said.

She looked over at Woody. "Hey mister buffalo husband, I need some lovin."

Woody looked pretty tired and didn't seem to be pleased at the prospect. "Yeah, sure darlin. It's time for us to turn in, see you all in the morning."

David and Jenny got up too. Jenny said, "Goodnight," and they headed off to their tent.

"We need to face it, it's time to sleep together," Matt said.

"Yeah, you have your cot and I have mine," Peggy said.

Matt helped pull Peggy to her feet and they moved off to the end tent. Matt glanced at his watch. It was ten thirty.

Peggy sat on the edge of her cot with her head in her hands.   "That woman is a monster," she said.

"There is something personal on this one, isn't there?" Matt asked.

Peggy looked up at Matt. "Yes, the buffalo she killed in San Francisco was my uncle," she said.

Matt moved over beside her and put his arms around her.

"You shouldn't have handled this one. You're too personally involved. Let's get some sleep and get out of here early tomorrow," Matt said.

Peggy nodded. Matt stood up and she lay back on her cot.

"Thanks, Matt. I would have enjoyed sleeping with you."

"Well you are. Only each on his own cot."

Matt lay back on his own cot. He could hear a coyote off in the distance. The wine, heavy meal and the outdoors took a toll on them both and they went quickly to sleep.

Sixteen

Matt was having a nightmare. There was this light and someone calling his name. Why is the bed so small? Was it dawn? Then he remembered he was in a tent, on a small cot by a desert lake with somebody shaking his shoulder and sticking that damn light in his face.

"Yeah, what?" he said.

"Matt, wake up. It's Woody. I need your help."

Matt glanced at his watch. It was three thirty.

"You getting up now?" Matt asked.

"No, it's Clarisa. I can't find her," Woody said.

"What?"

"We went to bed. She wanted to fool around. I was too tired. She got mad and said she was going to go out and sit by the fire. That was about eleven. I went to sleep. I woke up a little while ago and she wasn't on her cot. I checked the fire and she wasn't there either," Woody said.

Matt swung his legs over the edge of the cot, stretched and stood up.

"Let's check around. Maybe she just went to sleep out there somewhere," he said.

Matt followed Woody out toward the campfire, which was now only a few glowing embers.

"Why don't you get the fire going and I'll make a circle of the camp," Matt said.

"Alright, here's the flash light."

The flashlight was a strong one, so it illuminated a large area. Matt went down to the shore and the started a clockwise walk around the tent village. Even with the light, he stumbled and cursed as he fell down a small ravine. In a few minutes Woody had a respectable fire going again. The moon had gone down, so there was no help seeing there. Matt came back around to the shore

again. He had found nothing.

Woody came down to the shoreline.

"Where's my boat?" he said.

Matt looked out on the small cove. The only boat there was the Catalina 250.

"Could she have gotten on your boat and taken off?" Matt asked.

"I don't think so. As far as I know she doesn't know how to start it," Woody said.

"There may be a lot of things you don't know about Clarisa," Matt thought.

"I'm going to hike up to the point and see what I can see. Get the fire burning

brighter and maybe you should wake the others," Matt said.

"I went to wake Aaron first, but he and his gal were all naked and tangled,"

Woody said.

Matt walked up the shore on path that went up over some rocks and around the

stack of boulders that formed the point. He brushed into cactus and cursing came

up to a high point. From here he could overlook the little cove and the main part of

the lake. The sun was barely making some light in the east and it was easier to see.

Down to the south, maybe a mile or so he could just make out a boat, about thirty

yards off shore. It looked similar to Woody's boat.

Maybe Clarisa was angry, decided to sleep on the boat and somehow it wound up

down south. Matt turned and started back to the camp. Woody had the fire blazing

now and several of the others were gathered around the fire.

He was edging down a series of rocks when he glanced out in the water.

Something was there. He moved over in that direction. It was a body floating face

down. It was Clarisa. She had on only her panties and a bra. She was floating

about twenty-five feet off shore.

Matt sat down and stared at the scene. He oddly felt cheated. Someone or something had handed out justice to Clarisa before he could. All that work was for nothing.

He hated the next part. Usually, the police handed out the bad news about someone dying. He walked back to the campfire. He came up to Woody and said, "Let's go over here and sit down a minute, Woody."

"OK. You want to get a search organized?"

They sat down at the table where they had supper the night before.

"No, Woody. There's no easy way to say this. Clarisa is dead. She's over there floating just off shore. I'm sorry," Matt said.

"What?"

"Just a way down there by the point. I think your boat is down south a way," Matt said.

The other members of the party except Aaron and his date gathered around.

"What's wrong?" asked David.

"I'm sorry to tell you, David, but your sister is dead. She's floating in the water face down over by that point," Matt said.

"Are you sure she's dead?" Peggy said.

"I don't think there's any question. Why don't you go check?" Matt said.

Matt handed her the light and she turned to walk out to the point.

"We need to contact the police," Jenny said.

Matt went back to his tent, looked into his backpack and got out his cell phone. He dialed 911 and contacted the Maricopa County Sheriff's office.

The small rowboat putted up into the cove with Dirk, Juan and Carlita on board.

Dirk got out and came up to the group.

"You all are up early. Hard to sleep out here?" Dirk said.

"Clarisa's dead, Dirk," Woody said.

"Oh yeah?"

"Why don't you get Carlita to make us some coffee? We are going to be here a while," Matt said.

In about forty-five minutes the first sheriff's boat came around the point and put into shore. Soon after two other boats came in and a helicopter landed.

The sheriff's deputies took pictures of the body floating in the water and brought it in to shore. Woody was asked to make an ID by the deputy in charge.

Tom Thorn wore a tight fitting uniform over his two hundred and fifty pounds. He was balding and stoutly built. The uniform was crisply ironed and his belt buckled and shoes shined in the early morning light.

"I'm going to ask all you folks to just sit here around the fire and sip your coffee. I'll ask you each to come over, one at a time and sit with me over at the table there. I'll need a statement about what went on here. Thank you very much," Thorn said.

He started with Woody who was taking this well.

Matt sat beside Peggy and wondered what had happened.

Matt was the last one to be called over. He went over and sat down across the table from Thorn.

"Yes sir, your name please," Thorn said.

"Matt Dawson. I'm a private investigator looking into the death of the dead woman's previous husband."

Thorn raised his eyebrows. "Unusual for you to be on this camping trip, isn't it?"

"I suppose, but this is an unusual case," Matt said.

"What can you tell me about how this woman died?"

"She was fine when I last saw her though she was drunk. She and her husband went off to bed at ten thirty. They were in the tent off to the far right. Peggy and I were in the tent over on this end. About three thirty, Woody, Mr. Montana came over and woke me up. Said he couldn't find Clarisa. Wanted me to help find her. I

walked around the camp. Found nothing except that the motor boat was gone.
Then I went up on that point and I thought I saw the boat down south a couple of
miles. I was coming back to the camp when I spotted her floating, face down in the
water," Matt said.

Thorn grunted and kept scribbling his notes.

"I have been working on this case for a while so I know something about this
woman," Matt said.

"Is she someone I should know?" Thorn said.

"Only if you keep up with the Rich and Famous. Her previous name was Clarisa
Ashton, she's worth around two hundred million dollars," Matt said.

"What? And she's out here camping at Lake Pleasant?" Thorn said.

"Well, this is a top drawer camp site."

"Yeah. Could you come in to the office tomorrow and give me what you have on
this lady? Come in around ten. That ok?" Thorn asked.

"Sure, be glad to," Matt said.

The police had put yellow tape around the whole tent village. A couple of the
deputies went down and retrieved the motor boat and brought it back to the cove.
The deputies that had recovered the body put it in the helicopter. It had taken off
and returned by the time Thorn had finished talking to Matt.

Thorn gathered everyone around the campfire.

"Alright, I have your initial statements now. So you can all go home but I would
ask those people who live out of town to stay here in town a while until we can clear
this up," Thorn said.

"At this point what do you think happened to her?" David asked.

"It's too early to know for sure, but she might have decided to take a dip. Just
drowned because of what she had drunk the night before. I'll know more when we
get the autopsy done," Thorn said.

"Can we go back in the boat?" Woody asked.

"We'll have to keep that a while, Mr. Montana. The deputies will give you a ride back to the dock in their boats."

"How about the sailboat?" Matt asked.

"Yeah, you can take that back," Thorn said.

Peggy and Matt got their gear together, got back on the Catalina and shoved off. Matt started the motor and headed out of the cove and south, back to the dock.

The morning air was cool, especially out on the lake. Peggy huddled next to Matt in the cockpit. She was shivering.

"I feel strangely empty," Peggy said.

"I felt cheated when I saw her floating there," Matt said.

"I thought it would be important to me to see her pay for her crimes, but now…," Peggy said.

"Yeah, I know. I wonder if her trail of blood will ever be exposed to the light of day,"

Matt said.

Seventeen

Matt and Peggy finally got back to the hotel around noon. Matt was so tired he went up to his room, had a shower and dropped into bed.

Around four thirty he was awakened by the phone.

"Yeah?" Matt said groggily.

"Matt Dawson? This is Detective Kerns, San Francisco PD."

"Yeah Detective, what's up?"

"I've got news. The prints on the gate and some on the Miata match. Clarisa Ashton is the one who bought the car and ran down her husband that night," Kerns said.

Matt sat shaking his head.

"Isn't this the kind of thing you were hoping for? I'm contacting the Arizona authorities as soon as I can get an arrest warrant," Kerns said.

"Too late, Detective," Matt said.

"What? Why?"

"Clarisa's dead. She was found dead this morning, floating in a lake down here," Matt said.

Now it was Kern's turn to shake his head.

"Are you sure it's Clarisa?" Kerns asked.

"I'm the one that found her," Matt said.

"Oh. Well I guess that wraps it up," Kerns said.

"What will you do with your information?" Matt asked.

"I'll put it in the final report on this matter. Not much else I can do," Kerns.

"OK. Thanks for your efforts on this one Detective," Matt said.

"Thank you, Dawson. You're the one that broke the case. If you're ever up this way again, stop by," Kerns said.

"Thanks, I'll try to do that," Matt said.

He hung up the phone. Was this a dream or did this actually happen? He remembered the moment he saw Clarisa. He knew it was her. It wasn't that he liked Clarisa. She was a cold-blooded killer. But she was a worthy advisary. She was someone who had got away with murder for so long. No one had openly accused her of anything until now. Matt had put so much effort into this one, only to see her escape judgement. Or had she? Maybe someone had decided to bring her to justice in another way. Or did she just drown? She was certainly drunk enough to have done something stupid. That morning as they sat waiting out at the lake to be interviewed by the Sheriff's Deputy, they all were quite, lost in their own thoughts. Peggy seemed particularly shaken by the turn of events. Woody seemed nervous but not overly saddened by Clarisa's death. Dirk came over after he had helped pass out the coffee. He and Woody moved off to the side, talking softly between themselves. Aaron sat quietly, staring off into space. He was angry at something. Jenny and David chatted briefly about making some arrangements for Clarisa. Jenny was concerned about getting back to her work as she had a court date coming up in the next several days. Matt noticed that David's slacks were severely wrinkled, as if they had been wet and then allowed to dry into their current state. Matt was in a daze after being awakened so early, but he was enough awake to carefully note each of his fellow camper's mood and appearance. Was there anyone there that was truly sorry to see Clarisa dead?

Matt wondered if this would help or hurt Carson Ashton's effort to get control of the money. He put in a call to his office in San Francisco. When he came on the line he seemed tired and anxious.

"I've got some news for you," Matt said.

"Yes?"

"Clarisa is dead. She was found floating just off shore from the camp at the lake this morning," Matt said.

Carson looked out his window for a few moments. "How did she die?" he said quietly.

"Drowned presumably, I'm going in to talk to the investigators tomorrow morning, they should know more by then," Matt said.

"This could make things even more complicated," Carson said.

"I have another piece of news that might change things," Matt said.

"Really?"

"Detective Kerns called me, they now have proof, matching fingerprints on the Maria's Miata and the gate on the pier. They match Clarisa's prints," Matt said.

"Then she did kill my father?"

"And probably your mother," Matt said.

After a moment Carson said, "That bitch. I hope she suffered. At least the money is safe. This should decide the case. We should be able to have Clarisa's control of the money broken".

"What do you want me to do?" Matt said.

"Please get all of this to me in an updated report. You may have to come up here to testify," Carson said.

"Will Woody have access to the money now?" Matt asked.

"Good point. I need to get down there to be sure he doesn't move it off to Bermuda or something. I'll call you later when I think this through," Carson said.

"All right, I'll wait to hear from you. The police don't want anyone connected with the case leaving town yet, so I'll be here for a while," Matt said.

Matt got another call. It was from Frank.

"How was the camping trip?" Frank asked.

"Rather climatic. Clarisa is dead. I found her floating about twenty-five feet out and a little way off from the campsite this morning," Matt said.

"Wow. How did she die?"

"Drowned, I think. I'm getting together with the sheriff's deputy handling the case in the morning."

"Want to eat some dinner with us and tell all about it?"

"Sure, when?"

"Why don't you come over at six," Frank said.

Matt put down the phone. He still felt cheated somehow. He shook his head and headed over to Frank's hotel for dinner.

Again Frank had arranged for a table with a view. Out the window Squaw Peak stood out boldly in the rays of the red sunset to the west. Laura looked rested and fit, gracious as ever.

"How are you Matt? You look like you have been under bit of strain," Laura said after they had ordered their meals.

"Woody got me up around three thirty this morning to help him find Clarisa. I finally did. She was floating face down in the lake," Matt said.

"Oh, you poor dear. I guess this puts an end to this case," Laura said.

"Yes, but not just because of Clarisa's death. The San Francisco police now have evidence that could have proved she killed Devin Ashton," Matt said.

"Carson can use that to take control of the fortune," Frank said.

"Yes, I suppose so," Matt said.

Matt described the whole camping experience to Laura and Frank including all the sleeping arrangements.

"Is there anything going on between you and this insurance investigator," Frank asked.

"No, not really," Matt said.

"I talked to Quincey the other night," Frank said.

"Am I still verbotin as far as she's concerned?" Matt said.

"I think she has cooled down considerably," Frank said.

"What did she say? How did you happen to be talking to her?"

"She called me the other night while we were watching television. Said she just wanted to know how you were doing. I think she wanted to ask me for your phone number over here in Arizona, but she chickened out," Frank said.

"You should call her Matt," Laura said.

"I'll have to think about that," Matt said.

Their meals came and Frank brought Matt up to date on all the things he and Laura had been enjoying in Arizona. They had played golf, tennis and made a trip to the red rock country of Sedona and a short trip up to the Grand Canyon. Matt was still tired so after the meal he headed back to his hotel and sat on the bed. He looked at his watch. Quincey should be back at her condo by this time. It was late, but maybe she would talk to him. He called her number.

Her answering machine came on. Matt left a message.

"Quincy, this is Matt. I'm still in Arizona. I would like to talk to you. Could you call me at," He started looking for the hotel phone number.

Quincy picked up the phone. "Hello, Matt. I'm here."

"Oh, hi. I thought I'd call and see if you were still mad at me," Matt said.

"Well, I am, but I'm more mad at myself for being so self centered. You have a career too. Did you solve the case?" Quincy asked.

"It solved itself, more or less. I'm really sorry about the party. I wish I could have made it back," Matt said.

"Liar. You hate those things. I got over it. I went with our Program Director. We had a nice time."

"I miss you, Quincy," Matt said.

"I miss you too. When are you coming back?"

"In a few days. I have to check in with the fellow investigating Clarisa Ashton, now Clarisa Montana's death. It will probably take a few days to wrap this up," Matt said.

"Is that the heiress you told me about? The one with two hundred million dollars?"

"Yes, I found her floating in a lake early this morning," Matt said.

"This smells like a story," Quincy said.

"Most of the story may never be told. There is proof now that she had killed her last husband."

Matt could almost hear the wheels rumbling in Quincey's head. "I may want to talk to you some more about this tomorrow."

"OK. I'm beat right now. I'll talk to you tomorrow," Matt said.

"Matt, I'm so glad you called."

"Me too."

Matt put down the phone and fell over in bed.

Eighteen

The next morning Matt showered and dressed and went down for breakfast in the hotel coffee shop. He picked up an Arizona paper and ordered his breakfast. He noticed the headline splashed across the front page. "Ashton heiress found floating in Lake Pleasant." The story told of the presumably drowning death of Clarisa while on a camping trip with her husband and several others and the two hundred million-dollar estate that Woody Montana would now inherit. The story ended with the expectation that the investigating officer, Tom Thorn would hold a news conference later this week. Quincy was right. This would be the big story around town for a while.

At ten o'clock Matt pulled into the parking lot of the Maricopa County Sheriff's Office. The sheriff of Maricopa County was Joe Armondo. He was no ordinary sheriff. He was billed as the toughest sheriff in the country. Matt remembered reading an article in the San Diego paper detailing how Sheriff Joe had come down hard on criminals, fighting the lack of jail space by putting up surplus army tents. Matt glanced up at the billboard proclaiming 'Always room for one more in Tent City'. In order to save money he fed the inmates green baloney and kept them from escaping by issuing pink underwear. Sheriff Joe was the most popular politician in Arizona.

Matt had got up early that morning and had finished up the last chapter of his report for Carson Ashton. He printed out a copy and brought it along. He checked in at the reception desk and asked for Deputy Thorn. Security was tight. Besides the metal detectors, there was one Deputy who stood with his arms folded across his chest, carefully watching everyone that entered the office. Matt remembered that the newspaper article had said there had been several threats to Sheriff Joe's life. After passing though the metal detector, Matt found Tom Thorns' office. The sign said Commander Sheriff's Dept General Investigations Division.

Thorn looked up from his desk and said, "Oh, yes, Dawson. You're the guy that found the heiress in the lake. Come on in and have a seat."

"Good morning, Deputy," Matt said.

"I got a call about you this morning," Thorn said.

"Oh yeah?"

"Detective Kerns up in San Francisco filled me in on how you have been tracing the life story of our victim here, Clarisa Ashton Montana."

"Yes sir, I finished up the report on my investigation and I brought you a copy, in case you might be interested in her background." Matt slid the copy across Thorn's desk.

"I'm interested," Thorn said.

"Oh?"

"I got the preliminary report from the medical examiner. Clarisa Ashton was most likely killed. She had a gash on the top of her head. That didn't kill her, she drowned," Thorn said.

"Maybe she stumbled, hit her head on a rock and tumbled into the water," Matt said.

"Yeah, you would normally consider that except that the wound on her head is on the upper right side of the top of her head. If she had fallen, it would have been on her forehead, either right or left but not on the top. Plus, Dr. Ted, the examiner, said that it looked like the blow from a blunt instrument," Thorn said.

"Someone killed her," Matt said.

"That's what I think. I would like you to help me find out who did this, Mr. Dawson. Unfortunately, I can't pay you to help, but I can pick up some of your living expenses while you are here."

"Sure, I'd be glad to help. I do know something about everyone that was at the lake yesterday," Matt said.

"So, who do you think might have done this?"

"I hadn't considered this, Deputy. I thought she had drowned. She was quite drunk the last time I saw her," Matt said.

"As they say, you should follow the money. Mr. Montana now gets the two hundred million. I'd say he had a motive," Thorn said.

"It's possible. He says he didn't even know she was wealthy when he met her. After being around her even so short a time, I find that hard to believe."

"Wouldn't such a wealthy person get a prenuptial agreement signed if they married someone who wasn't also overly rich?" Thorn said.

"I think that usually would be the case, but Woody told me specifically that he did not sign one."

"What can you tell me about what went on after everyone went to bed the other night?" Thorn said.

"I was tired, too much to drink probably, though not close to the amount that Clarisa had drunk. I don't remember anything until Woody woke me at three thirty am."

"Was this insurance investigator, Peggy McClure asleep in her bed?"

"Yeah, I believe she was. As far as I know everyone was in their tent when Woody shook me awake."

"This is going to take some work. We need to find the murder weapon. But first, we need to take care of politics," Thorn said.

"How's that?"

"I don't know if you are familiar with our setup here, Mr. Dawson, but we have something of a Mexican standoff between our sheriff and the county attorney."

"I hadn't heard."

"They both are playing to the press, trying to get their side out. Sheriff Joe wants to meet with both of us and show his interest in the case. The county attorney tries to make the sheriff look bad every chance he gets."

"They are supposed to be on the same team," Matt said.

"You'd think. All Sheriff Joe's publicity and popularity galls Nick Mautley. Mautley is the county attorney. Why, we had a prison riot and Mautley was out there on the TV sympathizing with the inmates," Thorn said. He glanced at his watch.

"We need to get over there."

Matt followed Thorn down the corridor and put to the upper floor of the building. Sheriff Joe's office was grand with a large desk and state and the US flags behind and a wall full of mementos. Sheriff Joe was a middle aged, short bulldog a man with a down home self-deprecating demeanor. He stood up and shook Matt's hand across the desk.

"Mr. Dawson. So are you going to help us clear this one up?"

"Yes sir, I'll do my best," Matt said.

"Good, good. That San Francisco policeman is really a fan of yours. The press is already beating down my door. They're trying to do their job, but I can't get much else done except try to respond to their questions. Tom here says it's pretty definite that this heiress was killed. Have you got any prime suspects Tom?"

"Well sir, you always have to look at the husband first. I'm hoping Dawson here, can help me with checking out the other people on the trip as well. I'll need some overtime man hours looking for the murder weapon."

"You'll get whatever it takes. There's going to be a lot of looking over our shoulders here, so stick to the book. Look under every rock. Don't give our esteemed county attorney any opening to say we have bungled this one," Sheriff Joe said.

"Yes sir," Thorn said.

"Thanks for your help, Mr. Dawson," Sheriff Joe said.

"Glad to help," Matt said and they were ushered out of Sheriff Joe's office.

Matt and Thorn retraced their steps to Thorn's office. Thorn handed Matt the preliminary medical report on Clarisa.

"Have a seat in the waiting area there. I've got a few calls to make and I thought we would go out to the crime scene," Thorn said.

"Sure."

Matt found a sofa to sit on and looked over the few pages. The preliminary blood test showed that Clarisa had a 0.10 alcohol level. A graphic showed the location of the wound on her head. Death was due to drowning.

Matt cell phone announced itself.

"Dawson."

"Hi Matt. It's me. Where are you now?" Quincey asked.

"I'm at the Sheriff's Office. I'm going to be working with them for a while," Matt said.

"Great. Look, I talked to my station manager and he talked to ABC News. They want me to come over there and cover the story," Quincey said.

"Well, that's wonderful I guess."

"It's a big break for me Matt. I will get some national exposure."

"OK. Well, you can bunk in with me."

"Alright, that will be fun. I'm driving over there later this morning with a cameraman. I'll probably be at your hotel before your are," Quincey said.

"I'll call the front desk and have them give you a key," Matt said.

Matt gave Quincey directions to his hotel. He had just finished calling the front desk to tell them Quincey was coming when Thorn came out of his office. Matt hung up his phone and stood up.

"I'm ready," Matt said.

"Let's go," Thorn said and he led off up a flight of stairs.

"You have a parking lot upstairs?" Matt asked.

"No, the helicopter landing pad," Thorn said.

The helicopter rose quickly from the roof of the County Sheriff's office and turned

to the northwest. Matt noted the multilevel overpasses on the freeways.

"It's all beginning to look at lot like LA," Matt said.

"Not our fondest wish," Thorn said.

The city, ringed by mountains, stretched far to the north, with seemingly endless

subdivisions and malls. In the distance, Lake Pleasant came into view. The

helicopter flew up the eastern shore of the lake and into the cove where the Montana

camp was still set up. Woody's new boat bobbed by the shoreline.

The helicopter settled in a small flat area beside the lake and Thorn and Matt got

out. The engine was finally shut down and Matt noted the quiet. Only the gentle

lapping of the waves on the shoreline and the occasional screech of a bird.

"Quiet up here," Matt said.

"Yeah, only on weekdays though," Thorn said.

The yellow tape still circled the campsite and the deputy assigned to guard the

crime scene came over.

"Everything OK, Carl?" Thorn said.

"Been real peaceful here," Carl said.

"OK, Dawson. Show me where everyone was when you were awakened that

night," Thorn said.

Thorn followed as Matt walked over to what had been his and Peggy McClure's

tent.

"I was in that cot," Matt said.

Thorn sat on the cot.

"You couldn't see the campfire from here," Thorn said. He shifted over to the other cot.

"From here, I can see the campfire. Did you have the tent openings closed or shut?" Thorn asked.

"I think they all except Aaron's were open when I got up," Matt said.

"OK. Montana is here waking you up. What did you do?" Thorn said.

"I sat up. I pushed the light he had in my eyes away. Finally I understood what he wanted. We walked out to the campfire."

Thorn and Matt walked out to the charred remains of the fire.

"I told him to build up the fire. Maybe Clarisa was wandering around out there lost and she would see the fire and come in. Then I took the flashlight and went out to make a circle around the camp," Matt said.

Thorn followed as Matt retraced his steps. He remembered stumbling a couple of times. When he got back to the shoreline he said, "This is where we noticed that the boat was missing."

"Was that towel over there?" Thorn asked.

Matt looked a way down the shore. A towel was spread out on the ground.

"I don't remember seeing it, it might have been," Matt said.

They walked over to it.

"Any idea whose towel it was?" Thorn asked.

"I think it was one of the ones they were using on the motor boat when they were water skiing," Matt said.

"Who all was skiing?"

"Let's see. Aaron, his date, Jenny Paladora and David, Clarisa's brother got up at least once," Matt said.

Matt noticed the deputies had tagged an empty champagne bottle off to the right of the towel.

"You think that might have been the murder weapon?" Matt asked.

"No, it was something else more blunt. Not the right shape. We got some prints off that though. Who all were drinking champagne?" Thorn asked.

"Everyone around the campfire," Matt said.

"Who did the pouring?"

"Clarisa and Woody as I remember," Matt said.

They both walked back up the slope to the campfire.

"How light was it here that night?" Thorn asked.

"When I got up, it was pretty dark. Light from the stars was about all. I used a flashlight on my little tour around the campsite."

"Let's go up to the spot from where you saw the body," Thorn said.

When they had reached the spot he asked, "Do you remember how the motor boat was tied up? Was the bow line fastened to a tree or anything?"

"I had the sailboat pulled up on the shore. I think Woody had put a rock over the line to his boat. He should have put out an anchor to secure it somehow. The lake level must fluctuate."

"So where did you first see the body?"

"It was about over there, a ways down from the campsite."

"Somehow the boat came loose. It may have drifted around our around this point and down toward the dam," Thorn said.

"And if drifted that way, the body probably did as well," Matt said.

"Yes, so she was probably killed up closer to the camp," Thorn said.

They heard the sound of an outboard engine as a Sheriff's Boat came around the point and into the cove.

"That would be the divers," Thorn said and he started back down the trail toward the shoreline.

Matt followed Thorn back down to the cove shoreline. He was instructing the divers to search out in the cove.

"We are looking for a blunt instrument. Something large enough to whack someone over the head with," Thorn said.

The drivers turned away putting on their masks and started their job.

"It looks murky out there," Matt said.

"Yeah, but these boys are pretty good. They can usually find whatever their looking for. If it's out there," Thorn said.

"Anything on the Chriscraft that might be the weapon?" Matt asked.

"No. There is a tool box but nothing in it large enough to cause that wound. I think we have done all we can here. Hey Carl. Give me a call if they come up with anything."

Carl walked over. "Say Tom, I picked up something when I was coming up here this morning."

"Yeah?" Thorn said.

"I was talking to one of the Park Rangers. He said that he noticed that the late night fishermen were out here that night."

"Late night fishermen?" Thorn asked.

"There's a couple of guys that troll around the lake late at night. They think that's when the big ones bite. They come out maybe once or twice a week. They usually make a circle all around the lake goin in and out of each little bay," Carl said.

"He know their names or how to contact them?"

"No. I asked." Carl said.

"Maybe we'll put a piece in the paper and see if we can get them to contact us. Let's get on back, Dawson. I asked Mr. Ashton's date to come in to the office at about one," Thorn said.

Matt and Thorn got back into the helicopter for the ride back to the Sheriff's

Office.

Nineteen

Matt and Thorn came into the interview room where Melody Haskell sat there looking like a frightened rabbit. She had on her drab but tasteful business suit. She looked up and Matt thought she might begin to cry.

"Good afternoon, Miss Haskell. Thank you for coming in," Thorn said and he and Matt sat down.

"This won't take but a few minutes. We need to go over your statement from the other morning."

"Do I need a lawyer?" Melody asked.

"I wouldn't think so," Thorn said.

"They just want to go over what you told them before, Melody," Matt said.

"I didn't see anything," Melody said.

"OK. Let's see. Sometimes people remember little things that they forgot to mention. It says here that you and Aaron retired before the others," Thorn said.

"Yes, we went for walk down around the edge of the lake and we came back to our tent."

"What's the next thing you remember, that is after you fell asleep?" Thorn asked.

"Well, Mr. Montana came in to our tent. He shook Aaron and said that he couldn't find Mrs. Montana."

"Did either Aaron or you get up in the night? Before Woody woke you up?" Matt asked.

"Yes. Aaron got up once. To go to the bathroom I suppose," Melody said.

"About what time was that?" Thorn asked.

"I don't know. We had been asleep a while. Could have been midnight but I can't read my watch in the dark," Melody said.

"Did Aaron say anything about Clarisa to you, anything about the way she was acting a dinner?" Matt asked.

"No. Well, not really. I don't think he liked her much," Melody said.

"Why do you say that?" Thorn asked.

"I said something about how nice it was that she and Woody had invited me to go on the camping trip, and what a wonderful caring woman she was to work with the Indians and all," Melody said.

"What did Aaron say?" Matt asked.

"I don't understand it. I don't want to get Aaron in any trouble. I don't think he meant it. He might have had too much to drink," Melody said.

"What did he say, Melody?" Thorn asked.

"Well, he said she was a murdering bitch," Melody said.

Matt and Thorn glanced at each other.

"He was right, Melody," Matt said.

Thorn went through her previous statement and added the new facts she had remembered and let her get back to work.

Matt and Thorn spent the rest of the afternoon lining up interviews for the next day.

"Montana now has an attorney," Thorn said.

"Oh yeah?"

"I got a message from Mr. Conway Santeel. It says that any questioning of Mr. Woody Montana about the death of Clarisa Montana should be done in his presence. I'm setting up a meeting with them for nine tomorrow," Thorn said.

It was getting close to five when Matt said he was quitting for the day.

"Can you be back here at eight thirty or so we can be ready for the meeting with Woody and his attorney?" Thorn said.

"Yes sir, see you tomorrow."

It took Matt about forty five minutes for the drive back to north Scottsdale where his hotel was located. As he drove he was thinking of Quincey. She wasn't the easiest person to get along with, but he was fond of her. She might be out doing her TV reporter thing or out lounging by the pool. He parked and went in through the main entrance to the hotel, stopping by the front desk to see if Miss Ferris had checked in.

"Yes sir. She came in about an hour ago," the front desk clerk said.

"Matt went up in the elevator and went down the hall to his room. He put in his magnetic striped room key and after a couple of tries managed to get the lock to operate. He pushed the door open but the chain was on the door so that it would only open up a short way.

"Quincey, it's me. Are you in there?"

Quincey pushed back the door and took off the chain. She pulled it partially open and stuck her head out around it. Matt could see she wasn't wearing a blouse.

"So who want's to know?" she said.

Matt laughed and pushed open the door. She didn't have a stitch on.

Matt closed the door behind him and took her in his arms.

"That's what I call a sensational hello," Matt said.

After a deep kiss Quincey said, "I thought you'd never get here."
They both tore at Matt's clothes as they headed for the bed. Make up sex was the best.

The next morning Matt and Quincey were up early and were the first customers of the hotel coffee shop. Matt grabbed a newspaper and they settled into a booth for some breakfast. The banner headline said "Heiress Murdered at lake."

Quincey saw the headline and said, "Matt, you didn't tell me see was murdered."

"I had other things on my mind."

"How did she die?" Quincey asked.

"Blow to the head and then she drowned," Matt said.

"This is going to be really big," Quincey said.

"Rather sad. I don't think anyone at the lake that was sorry that she was dead," Matt said.

"Didn't you tell me that you suspected her of killing several people including her previous husband?"

"Yes. The San Francisco police now have the proof that she did in fact run her husband down in a parking lot."

Quincey produced a notebook and started making notes pumping Matt for the names of the contacts in San Francisco and some of the details of the other killings that Clarisa might have done.

"Hi, Matt."

Matt looked up. Peggy McClure had come into the dinning room and was giving him a special smile.

"Oh, hi Peggy. Peggy, this is Quincey Ferris. She's a TV reporter. Quincy this is Peggy McClure, the insurance investigator I was telling you about," Matt said.

"Obviously you didn't tell me everything about her," Qunicey said.

Matt had his mouth open trying to think what to say.

"I understand you're working with the Sheriff's Office now so guess I'll be seeing you later. I have an appointment to go in any talk to Deputy Thorn," Peggy smiled and she moved off to another table.

"Yeah, see you then," Matt said.

Quincey had several other questions on her lips but decided to wait until later to go into it. When they had finished their breakfasts, Quincey said, "I'll be working out of the local ABC affiliate. Call me on my cell phone when you find out when the Sheriff's office is going to have a press conference. Got to go."

"Me too," Matt said and he left some cash for the bill.

Matt arrived at the Maricopa County Sheriff's Office at about eight fifteen and was shown into a large conference room. Tom Thorn was sitting beside another man in an expensive suit. There was a pile of papers before him.

"Matt, good morning. This is our Country Attorney, Mr. Nick Mautly," Thorn said.

Mautly grudgingly stood up and shook Matt's hand. "And you are?" Mautly asked. Mautly was a short man with balding blond hair and a small mustache.

"Matt Dawson, Mr. Mautly."

"Matt's a private investigator that we have asked to help us on this case. He's been tracking the victim Clarisa Montana, for several months," Thorn said.

"Tracking her?" Mautly asked.

"The San Francisco police now have the evidence to prove she had killed her last husband with a car," Matt said.

"And it probably wasn't her first murder," Thorn said.

"All that doesn't matter now. We have her murder to deal with. I read over your preliminary report Thorn, this Montana fellow was twenty years younger than the victim?" Mautly said.

"Yes, they had been married only a short time," Thorn said.

"And she was struck by a blow to the head and then she drowned. She must have been in the water this happened. Do you have a time of death?" Mautly said.

"Around midnight is what they're telling me now," Thorn said.

The door opened to the conference room and a secretary put her head in the room. "Mr. Montana and his attorney are here, Mr. Thorn."

"Have them some on in," Thorn said.

Woody Montana and his lawyer entered the room. Mautly stood up and reached across the table and shook the lawyer's hand.

"Conway, good to see you," Mautly said.

"And you, Mr. County Attorney. How have you been Nick?" Conway Santell said.

Santeel had the look of a successful lawyer. He had on a fine expensive tailored suit, a shirt with only a hint of a pattern in it and a carnation in his buttonhole, which somewhat marred the general effect.

"Fine. Mr. Montana, I'm Nick Mautley, Maricopa County Attorney." Mautley shook Montana's hand.

"Yes sir. Glad to meet you," Woody said.

"We need to go over your statement from the other morning and see if you can add anything that might help us clear this all up. I think you know Mr. Dawson here," Thorn said.

"Sure, mornin' Matt."

"Good morning, Woody," Matt returned.

"Mr. Dawson was on the camping trip as well the other morning?" Santeel asked.

"Yes sir," Matt said.

"Mr. Montana, you're aware that it appears that your wife was killed by a blow to the head and then she drowned?" Mautley asked.

"Yes sir. I read the paper," Woody said.

"There might be some other interpretation of those facts," Santeel said.

"No doubt. Could you tell us what you think happened Mr. Montana?" Thorn asked.

"I don't know. The last time I talked to Clarisa she was fine, though maybe few sheets to the wind," Woody said.

"Let's take it from the top, Mr. Montana. Could you go over what you know to have happened when you decided to turn in the other evening?" Thorn said.

"We had a few bottles of champagne around the fire with everyone except Aaron and his date. They had turned in earlier. About ten thirty we decided to turn in. I was real tired and just wanted to sleep. Clarisa said she wasn't ready to go to sleep and so she went out to sit around the campfire some more," Woody said.

"Was she angry with you at that point, Mr. Montana?" Mautley asked.

"Well, a little. She wanted to fool around but I was too tired," Woody said.

"What time was this?"

"Must have been around eleven," Woody said.

"Did you see anyone else out by the campfire?" Thorn asked.

"Naw, I flopped over and went right to sleep," Woody said.

"Did you get up in the night at any point?" Thorn asked.

"It was after three when I woke up and glanced over at Clarisa's cot. It was empty. I looked at my watch and realized that she should have been in bed by now. I got concerned and got up. I went out to the campfire. It had died down to a few coals. It was pitch dark so I went back to the tent and got the flashlight. I went back out there with it but I still didn't see her," Woody said.

"You hadn't gotten out of bed at anytime before this?" Mautley asked.

"No sir. Well wait. I did go out once right after Clarisa stomped off to pee," Woody said.

"Did you see her sitting down at the campfire at that point?" Thorn said.

"I don't remember even looking. I was real tired. I went back and hit the sack," Woody said.

"Mr. Montana, were you a wealthy man? I mean before you married Clarisa," Mautley asked.

"I have my business and my little ranch property. I owe some to the banks but I had a little net worth I suppose," Montana said.

"Not nearly as great as that you had after you married Clarisa?" Mautely asked.

"No sir. I guess not," Woody said.

"I understand you didn't realize how wealthy Mrs. Ashton was when you married her. Is that correct?" Thorn asked.

"No sir. I didn't think she was penniless but I never figured her for such a humongous pile of cash," Woody said.

"Did you sign a prenuptial agreement?" Mautley asked.

"No sir, we talked about it. I thought she was worried about protecting my little estate for my daughter. The Ashton children weren't hers. I don't think she thought much of any of them except Aaron," Woody said.

"Mr. Montana, were you still in love with your wife?" Mautely asked.

"Certainly, we'd been married only a short time," Woody said.

"There was twenty years difference in your ages," Mautely said.

"Yes, but I been with a lot of the younger ones. I wanted someone that was stable and had a good heart. Clarisa had a whole lot of causes that she cared deeply for. I respected her for that," Woody said.

"Mr. Montana, would you be willing to take a lie detector test?" Mautely asked.

Woody glanced at his lawyer and leaned over as Santeel whispered in his ear. Woody whispered back a reply and then Santeel must have repeated his first advice.

"Mr. Montana will decline the offer of taking a lie detector examination," Santeel said.

"May I say something?" Matt asked Thorn.

"As long as it's on the subject," Mautly said.

"Woody, did you talk to Aaron about what I had told him about Clarisa?" Matt asked.

Santeel leaned over and whispered in Woody's ear.

"I'm advising Mr. Montana to not say anything further on this matter. He has given you all the information about what he knows about his wife's death. I believe this interview is now complete," Santeel said.

Santeel stood up and almost pulled Woody to his feet. Woody looked shocked and disoriented.

"Gentlemen," Santeel said and they left the room.

"It must have been something I said," Matt said.

"What did you say to this Aaron?" Mautely asked.

"I let him read my report on Clarisa that I had prepared for Carson Ashton. We needed Aaron to be more forthright about what had happened on the night his father was killed," Matt said.

"So he knew you suspected Clarisa Montana of killing his father?" Mautley said.

"And his mother. And the other husband she married," Matt said.

"He might have passed that along to Montana," Thorn said.

"Did Aaron believe you?" Mautley said.

"I think so. Especially from some the things he said after he had seen the report," Matt said.

"Did he agree to testify against Clarisa?" Mautley said.

"I never got a chance to find out," Matt said.

"Things are usually pretty simple when it comes down to it. I would like you to get a picture of Mr. Montana's financial standing prior to his marrying Mrs. Ashton, Thorn," Mautley said.

"Yes sir," Thorn said.

"We need to nail this one down pretty fast. Try to remember the rules of evidence. We don't need any more mistakes on this one," Mautley said.

Thorn didn't respond to that one but the frown on his face said volumes. Mautley stuffed his papers in his briefcase and left.

"Real team player," Matt said.

"Exactly," Thorn said.

Twenty

Matt left the sheriff's office to meet Frank for lunch. He had called and they selected a restaurant in downtown Phoenix at the Arizona Center. I was an office building complex that included an upscale retail area with several restaurants. Matt found a spot in the parking building and went down to walk through the garden in front of the center. A variety of palms and water fountains gave the place a cool feeling. Matt saw that Frank already had a table out on the patio of Sam's Place.

"Hi Frank. How are you?" Matt said.

"Great. You seem to have a little more quickness to your step. Did Quincey come over to Arizona?" Frank asked.

"You are the best detective," Matt said.

"That's great that she could take time off work to come over here," Frank said.

"Oh, no. She's on an assignment. Reporting of the heiress' murder for ABC news now," Matt said.

"Really? Good for her. Murder? I thought you said Clarisa drowned?" Frank said.

"Yes, after a blow to the head."

"I got concerned phone call from Mr. Martin C. Justin again," Frank said.

"Oh yeah?"

"It seems that Carson has access to all of Clarisa's accounts and holdings. He found out that Mr. Montana has moved a chunk of the money to an offshore account in the Cayman Islands. Carson and his sister, and Justin for that matter, are very upset," Frank said.

"Woody is moving fast," Matt said.

"I got rooms for them all at the Biltmore. They are flying in this afternoon and I'm going to meet them. Carson asked if you could set up a meeting for them with Mr. Montana and his lawyer. He is not returning Carson's calls," Frank said.

"I can try. Woody may not talk to me either now that I'm kind of on the other side, helping the Sheriff's Office," Matt said.

"Give it a try anyway," Frank said.

"OK. Would you like to do something on this case? I have job in mind that might be right down your alley," Matt said.

"Sure. I think I have looked at all the cactus I want to for a while," Frank said.

"This might involve some more of that. One of the Sheriff's Deputies got a tip from the Lake Pleasant Park Ranger that there are a couple of fishermen that come out to the lake once or twice a week and spend the night trolling around the whole lake. The Park Ranger didn't know their names. I was thinking that if a Park Ranger knows these guys then maybe someone else up at the lake would as well."

"OK. I don't know why that's up my alley but I'll see what I can do," Frank said.

"Well, you fish off that boat of yours," Matt said.

"I see. When do you think you can talk to Montana?"

"I'll try to see him this afternoon."

Their lunch came and Matt filled Frank in on the progress of the investigation into Clarisa's murder.

"What is Laura up to?" Matt asked.

"This is her spa day. She's getting a massage, a facial and then a new hair do, the works."

"Tell her, hi. Maybe we can all get together, if I can get Quincey away from the news business for a while. I better get back."

"OK. I'll call you later. Carson and the others may want to get together with you."

Matt arrived back at Tom Thorn's office as he came out the door.

"Aaron Ashton is waiting in conference room three. Let's see what he has to say," Thorn said.

Aaron had on an expensive designer label sports shirt and slacks. He sat comfortably with his legs crosses with an air of being mildly annoyed at being kept waiting. He wiggled his tasseled, soft calf skin loafers vigorously.

"Good afternoon, Mr. Ashton. Thanks for coming in. I have a few questions about the camping trip and of course your step mother's death," Thorn said.

"Certainly, deputy. I want to cooperate in any way I can," Aaron said.

"Hello, Aaron," Matt said.

"Hello, Matt."

"Scanning back over your initial statement I see that you went soundly to sleep and don't recall anything until you were awakened early the next morning by Mr. Montana," Thorn said.

"That's right."

"Miss Haskell said you got up at least once in the night. Possibly to relive yourself," Thorn said.

"Who? Oh, Melody. Well, yes, maybe I did. I got up once. I put on my sandals and went around to the back of the tent. I was only up for a few minutes," Aaron said.

"What time was that?" Thorn asked.

"I think it was around midnight. I did look at my watch now that I think about it. Yes, it was around midnight."

"What did you see while you were out there?" Thorn asked.

"It was dark. I didn't see anything, only the coals of the campfire were visible. I did hear voices though," Aaron said.

"What voices?" Thorn said.

"I can't be sure. One was louder than the other. They were out there somewhere on or near the water. I thought it was a pair of drunken fishermen or something. Voices carry over water."

"Could one of the voices have been your step mother?" Thorn said.

"I had assumed that she was in her tent. But, yes, it might have been."

"Did you go down to investigate?" Thorn said.

"No. I was tired, sleepy. I just wanted to get back to bed," Aaron said.

"Did you catch any of the conversation?" Thorn continued.

"No. Just a loud laugh," Aaron said.

"Mr. Ashton, I wonder if you can tell us about another subject which you might think is personal as far as Mrs. Montana is concerned. It's something we will eventually find out about so you needn't be concerned about revealing things we will eventually know," Thorn said.

"I'd be glad to help in any way I can."

"Do you know how Mr. and Mrs. Montana handled their financial affairs?" Thorn asked.

"I don't know what aspect you are interested in but the basic situation was that Clarisa was in tight control of all the money," Aaron said.

"How was that?"

"In theory, half of everything was Woody's but in reality they had two bank accounts, his and hers. She would dole out a little money to him every so often to keep him happy. But, he needed some more serious funds, he is deeply in debt. I think he may have to declare bankruptcy. I know she would let that happen because it happened to me. To her, all the money was hers to spend. She was the only one with the divine guidance on what was worthy or not. More than half of the estate is in real estate. Not liquid. Another large portion is in stocks and other more liquid investments. To make Woody feel ok she put his name on one investment account, but the account manager would only take instruction from her. So, the only way Woody was going to get at the cash was if he divorced her," Aaron said.

"Or killed her," Matt said.

"Mr. Dawson here tells me that he showed you his report on Clarisa Ashton and the probability that she had killed each of her previous husbands, including your father. Is that true?"

"Yes, and she killed my mother as well," Aaron said.

"How could you live with her if you knew this?" Thorn asked.

"I can't understand that myself. I only realized this when Dawson showed me the report. It merely confirmed suspicions I had before, but it was like waking up and realizing I had been a fool as far as she was concerned," Aaron said.

"Were you angry enough to have killed her, Aaron?" Thorn said.

"No, no. I was angry. I still am angry. Wouldn't you be? But I've never been decisive enough to do anything like that. I didn't kill her."

"Did you talk to Mr. Montana about the report?" Thorn asked.

"Yes. Yes, I did. At first he didn't believe me, then I think maybe he did."

"Why is that?" Thorn asked.

"He made a crack that if he didn't service her she might bump him off," Aaron said.

"At one point you said something intemperate yourself, didn't you Aaron?" Thorn asked.

"What that?"

"You told Melody that Clarisa was a murdering bitch," Thorn said.

Aaron hung his head. "Yes, I did, but I didn't kill her."

Thorn had Aaron's statement edited and had him sign the new version. Aaron left the Sheriff's Office in a frightened and confused state.

Matt and Thorn returned to Thorn's office.

"That puts a lot of light on the situation. How did you read Woody Montana's feeling as to his wife, Dawson?" Thorn asked.

"It might be colored by my own distaste for the woman, but he was going overboard to please her while on the other hand she was just being her normal bitchy self. Maybe that's only natural if she represented the answer to your financial problems," Matt answered.

Thorn's phone rang.

"Tom Thorn."

Thorn listened for a few seconds.

"Great, get it back here are soon as you can," he said and hung up.

"They found a large wrench out in that little cove. It might be the murder weapon, it was big enough," Thorn said.

"We need to tie it into the group somehow," Matt said.

"Do you remember seeing a large wrench?" Thorn asked.

"No. But, I wasn't on board the motor boat. I do remember Woody having a problem with his motor at one point during the afternoon. It looked like he was using some tool to fix it," Matt said.

"I've got the brother and Jenny Paladora coming in for an interview in fifteen minutes. They were on the Chriscraft. Let's see if they can tie it in," Thorn said.

Matt and Thorn entered the same conference room where Jenny Paladora and David Wilkes were seated. Thorn went into his standard spiel.

"Thanks so much for coming down. I have a few questions regarding your sister's death, Mr. Wilkes. And, Mrs. Paladora, I understand that Clarisa had been your friend since high school," Thorn said.

"Yes. Though I hadn't seen much of her since that time until recently," Jenny said.

"Mr. Wilkes, what can you tell me about that night, after you retired for the evening?" Thorn asked.

"Not much. I did get up once to relive myself. The next thing I remember was Woody shaking my shoulder and saying he couldn't find Clarisa," Wilkes said.

"When did you get up?" Thorn asked.

"I don't know exactly."

"Was it after you went to sleep, around midnight or just before you were awakened by Mr. Montana?"

"I don't know. I was tired from the boating activities. I don't normally have that much exercise. It's all a blur," David said.

"Was Miss Paladora on her cot when you went out?" Thorn asked.

"Why yes, of course."

"Miss Paladora, did you get up and go outside the tent after you had gone to bed that evening?" Thorn asked.

"No. I went to sleep. I don't remember anything until Woody came in," Jenny answered.

The door to the conference room opened and Thorn's secretary poked her head into the room.

"Bill Evans said I should bring this to you, Commander Thorn," she said.

"OK. What have you got?" Thorn asked.

The secretary opened the door fully and came in with a large clear plastic envelope containing an approximately eighteen inch long wrench. Thorn placed it in the middle of the table.

"Thanks, Helen," he said.

"Mr. Wilkes, have you seen this wrench before?" Thorn asked.

"May I pick it up?" Wilkes asked.

"Certainly."

Wilkes picked up the wrench and examined it carefully.

"I think this is the tool Woody was using," Wilkes said.

"When was that?" Thorn asked.

"Out on the lake. One of the motor mounts came loose. The thing was thrashing about. Woody killed the motor, got out the toolbox and used this thing to tighten the bolts. Fixed it fine. What's special about this?" Wilkes asked.

"It may have been used in the murder," Thorn said.

Wilkes placed the envelope back on the table as if were truly evil.

"How about you, Ms. Paladora. Do you remember this being on Mr. Montana's boat?" Thorn asked.

"Yes, I believe that it or one that looked like that was the tool Mr. Montana used to fix the problem with the engine," Jenny said.

"Mr. Wilkes, I need to ask you about some rather personal financial matters. We can do this without Ms. Paladora being present if you prefer," Thorn said.

Wilkes glanced at Jenny. "No, that's alright, Jenny and I are quite close."

"I understand that you have recently been involved with a new stock offering. Clarisa Ashton made a sizeable investment, which allowed this to proceed. Is that true?" Thorn asked.

"Yes. It was only the initial phase that was completed, however."

"I further understand that the offering was not really successful in that the shares are now only selling for a fraction of their original offering price," Thorn said.

"That true at the moment. Again, that was because a secondary placement never occurred," Wilkes said testily.

"And Clarisa was the one that was supposed to pick that up?"

"Well, yes. She would have done it in the long run though," Wilkes said.

"You were pretty angry with your sister for not coming through for you, weren't you Mr. Wilkes?"

"I was angry, yes."

"Enough to kill her?" Thorn said.

"No. Never," Wilkes said.

"David, on another subject. I noticed that your slacks had been wet. The ones you were wearing on the morning that Commander Thorn talked to us at the lake. How did that happen?" Matt asked.

"Oh that. Quite embarrassing really. You remember that I was out watching the eagle's dive for food. Well, after supper and our little campfire session, I remembered a bird book I had brought out. I thought I might see what it had to say about eagles. It was still on the boat so I went out to get on board and retrieve it. I slipped into the water in the process and my slacks got all wet. I went back to the tent and changed into my shorts and hung my pants up to dry," Wilkes said.

"Can you verify this, Ms. Paladora?" Thorn asked.

"Oh, well, no I think I was out of the tent, getting ready to go to bed myself at that point," Jenny said.

"One more point. I understand that you are in Clarisa Montana's current will. It that correct?" Thorn said.

"I think that is true. The will hasn't been read yet though," Wilkes said.

"Have you any idea who would want to kill your sister, Mr. Wilkes?" Thorn asked.

Wilkes thought a moment. He glanced at Jenny. "No. I really don't."

"OK. That's all I have for now. Please don't leave town for another few days. I think we should have this wrapped up by then. Thanks again for coming down," Thorn said.

As Matt and Thorn were walking back toward Thorn's office Matt said, "Carson Ashton has asked me to see if I can set up a meeting with Woody Montana. I think the only way to do that is to go out there and see if I can talk to him," Matt said.

"Alright, but keep to that subject. Don't let on about anything else about the case," Thorn said.

"Right," Matt said.

Twenty One

Matt took the freeway that looped around to the east of Phoenix and Scottsdale.

How many of the happy campers at the lake could or would have killed Clarisa? The

obvious choice was Woody. Was he faking his fondness for the dragon? What were

he and Dirk discussing that morning at the campsite as they were waiting to be

interviewed by Thorn? Brother David had his problems with his sister and his story

about the shriveled up slacks seemed unlikely. Did he get wrinkled drowning his

sister? Jenny Paladora might have something against Claris, but it was so long ago.

Aaron was a prime suspect. He might have the emotion to finally try to rectify his

error in being part of Clarisa's retinue. Even Peggy McClure could have a motive of

vengeance.

As he neared Woody's Buffalo Ranch, Matt saw a TV remote unit and small group

of people gathered below one of the buffalo statues guarding the entrance to the

Montana house. He parked at the end of the block and walked toward the group.

Quincey was in the middle of a take, holding the mike in front of her and talking a

steady stream into the camera.

One of the TV technicians put up his hand to stop Matt from getting too close to

Quincey and the cameraman.

"... and ABC News has learned that the heiress' fortune is in the range of two

hundred million dollars. Up to this point, the former Mrs. Devin Ashton's new

husband of only a few months and twenty years her junior has not made a

statement to the press," Quincey was saying.

Matt noticed Dirk Smith climb over the automatic gate stretched between the buffalo

statues and begin advancing toward Quincey.

Quincey turned as she noticed him coming toward her.

"Alright, I want you all to clear out of here. This is private property," Dirk said

menacingly.

"Hello, I'm Quincey Ferris, ABC News and you are on the air. What is your name sir?" Quincey said.

Dirk raised his hand as if he was going to slap the mike out of Quincey's hands.

"Get the hell out. Now," he said.

"Are you Mr. Montana?" Quincey asked.

Dirk swung out and sent the mike flying. For once Quincey looked a little shaken. Matt moved around the people standing in front of him and got between Quincey and an angry Dirk Smith.

"Let's play it cool, Dirk," Matt said.

Dirk responded with a roundhouse right that caught Matt squarely on the chin. Matt had taken Karate lessons and it was at times like this that he kept reminding himself he needed some more. Dirk had plenty of lessons while he was in the slammer. Dirk rushed at him as he regained his feet and Matt managed a move that flipped Dirk over on his back. Matt put his left knee in Dirk's throat.

"Like I said, let's be cool, Dirk," Matt said.

"You can let him up now. Dirk this isn't helping. Stay down there until you get your wind back," Woody said. He had come down the driveway and now was standing beside Matt. He picked up Dirk's hat moved it to his left hand and picked up Quincey's microphone.

Matt stood up and offered Dirk a hand up. Woody handed Quincey her microphone. She blew in it a couple of times and indicated to the cameraman to start shooting again.

"Mr. Montana, Quincey Ferris, ABC News. Have you any comments on how the police are handling the investigation into your wife's death?"

Woody seemed overwhelmed by the camera and lights.

"I didn't kill my wife. We had been married only a couple of months ago," Woody said.

"Is it true that you have declined to take a lie detector test?" Quincey said.

"I shouldn't be talking about this," Woody said.

Matt took Woody's arm and led him back to the gate. Woody reached down and brought out a control that opened the gate and he and Woody walked back toward the house.

Dirk got up and kept the surge of people standing outside the property from following.

"Woody, I need to talk to you for a few minutes," Matt said.

"My lawyer said I wasn't to talk to anyone, maybe especially you," Woody said.

"This isn't about the investigation. Carson Ashton asked me to see if you and he could sit down and discuss the situation," Matt said.

"The money you mean?" Woody asked.

"You're probably right, but maybe you two can come to an agreement which might help you with the press," Matt said. He knew he was reaching for a reason.

"I'm not trying to get anything that isn't legally mine."

"It couldn't hurt to talk," Matt said.

"OK. When and where?"

"How about ten tomorrow morning. I'll get a conference room at the Biltmore," Matt said.

"Fine."

"Thanks, Woody," Matt said and he turned and walked back to the entrance where Quincey was once again recording another report.

As a visiting guest Quincey had received a gift from the local ABC affiliate, tickets to their suite at the Bank One Ballpark for that evening. Quincey and Matt drove over to the Biltmore and met Frank, Laura, Carson Ashton and his sister Beth Agasture in the lobby. Frank had hired a limo to take the group down to the baseball game. Mr. Martin Justin, the Managing Director of the Children's Cancer Hospital had come to town as well, but he was having dinner with another charity hospital administrator

colleague. Carson Ashton seemed somber and brooding as he shook hands with

Matt.

"Hello Mr. Dawson, I hope you can help us right this situation," Carson said.

"Yes sir, I hope so too," Matt said.

They all piled into the long white limousine and the driver headed off down to the

ballpark. Beth Agasture didn't seem in any better mood and snapped back at Frank

when he inquired if she liked baseball.

"I've been to most of the top flight major league parks, but this hardly seems the

time for a baseball game now."

"Sometimes it's best to try to get your mind off things when you're under a

strain," Laura said always trying to be the peacemaker.

Frank and Matt tried to relieve the strained atmosphere by reviewing where the

Diamondback's were in the western division of the National League. Tonight, they

were playing the LA Dodgers. It didn't seem to help. Carson stared out the window

and Beth sat glowering with her arms folded.

They finally reached the ballpark and the driver let them off at the entrance that

allowed them to take the elevator up to the suite level. When they reached the

suite, waiters came by for drink orders and they helped themselves to a fine buffet

including salmon and prime rib as the main entrées. They had finished eating when

the Star Spangled Banner was played. Matt was getting another beer when Carson

called him over to the far corner of the suite for a little one on one.

"Matt, can I call you that? Do you think this Woody Montana killed Clarisa?"

Carson asked.

"There is some circumstantial evidence toward that theory, but I don't know,"

Matt said.

"What would that be?"

Matt wondered if he was violating any understanding he had with Thorn. The fact was that the Sheriff's Department wasn't paying Matt. Carson Ashton was paying him, plus Carson was not a suspect.

"Montana is on the financial ropes, though maybe not now that he has his hands on a least part of the money," Matt said.

"Yes, a substantial part, over twenty million dollars. Why was there a problem with money before Clarisa was killed?" Carson asked.

"She kept tight control on all the funds. She put Woody's name on the account he just moved. But the broker, I'm told, would only take orders from Clarisa on that account. Everything else was in her name only. In a divorce he could have got something but until recently, he only had what she doled out to him and apparently his buffalo business was headed into the toilet," Matt said.

"If he knew her history he might well have killed her in self defense," Carson said.

"He did hear about my report, I don't know if he believed it or not," Matt said.

"If he did kill her, that would invalidate this new will of hers. I feel certain we can prove in time that she wasn't entitled to anything herself, but time is the issue. I would like you to keep investigating this case for me Dawson. If it can be shown that he's guilty of this then that's one more aid to preserving the money," Carson said.

"I told the Sheriff I would help. If it doesn't interfere with finding the truth I don't see why I can't keep working for you," Matt said.

"Fine. I would like periodic updates as you have done in the past. Frank told me that you did secure a meeting with Mr. Montana tomorrow," Carson said.

"Yes, I told him to be at the Biltmore at ten. We need to arrange for a conference room," Matt said.

The crowd roared. The Diamondbacks had loaded the bases in what was now the bottom of the first inning. Matt and Ashton moved out to watch some of the game. Quincey was really into baseball and was routing for the Dodgers since if they got a win, her Padres would move up a rank in the Western Division. It was an exciting and close game with the Diamondback winning in the tenth with a wild pitch from the Dodger's closer.

Twenty Two

Carson Ashton had hired a local attorney, William Bental. The next morning at ten fifteen, Bental, Matt, Frank, Carson Ashton, Beth Agasture and Martin C. Justin sat across a polished oak table from Woody Montana and his lawyer, Conway Santeel. The Phoenix Mountains with Squaw Peak dazzling in the morning sun stood out against a cloudless sky in the picture window of the second floor conference room at the Biltmore. The hotel staff had served coffee, Danish and bagels and left the room. Carson spoke first.

"I want to thank you both for coming in to meet us. It is my hope that we can come to some agreement that will avoid extended litigation," Carson said.

"I don't see why there should be any litigation. My client is clearly the beneficiary of Clarisa Montana's will. The will is going to be probated Monday morning in the court of Justice Harvey J. Friedhower," Conway said.

"Wasn't he in your firm at one time, Conway?" Bental asked.

"Well, yes, but that is neither here nor there," Conway said.

"You're trying to get away with stolen goods Mr. Montana. Clarisa stole this money from us," Beth said.

"We were lawfully married, and she left it to me," Woody said.

"It wasn't hers though, Mr. Montana. The police now have evidence that she killed my father. That will invalidate her receiving anything from my father's estate. We will bring that evidence forward in any court proceeding," Carson said.

"What that evidence is and whether it will stand up is a matter yet to be decided," Conway said.

"The evidence is strong and convincing. But, I would rather come to a settlement that would have your client relinquish any claim he might have on the estate save for a small portion," Carson said.

"How small a portion?" Conway asked.

"We can discuss that with a smaller group perhaps but certainly less than he has already misappropriated," Carson said.

Conway turned to Woody and that had a whispered conference.

"We will take your offer under advisement and I'll get back to you or Mr. Bental in a couple of days," Conway said. He and Woody got up and left the room.

"Why should we give them a red cent?" Beth asked Carson.

"Wouldn't you rather get most of the money for certain than to put your fate in the hands of some jury? Remember, OJ walked out free. Trials are not totally predictable," Carson said.

"I think the offer is a prudent move," Bental said.

"If you get the money back, are you still going to honor your father's wishes as far as the hospital is concerned?" Justin asked.

"Certainly," Carson said.

It looked as if Beth was less sure.

"We need to be at the probate hearing, Bental," Carson said.

"Right, I'll have a motion to contest and come by and pick you up first thing Monday morning," Bental said.

They all moved out into the hall and to the elevator. In the lobby Matt pulled Frank aside.

"How's the fishing coming?"

"I'm going out to try my luck this morning," Frank said.

"Alright, give me a call on my cell phone if you find anything," Matt said and he hurried out to the parking lot for the drive down to the Sheriff's office.

When Matt reached the Sheriff's Office Thorn's secretary told him that the next interviewee had already arrived. He was to join them in the same interview room. Matt knocked and went in. The interviewee was Peggy McClure.

"Hi Matt," Peggy said. "It was so nice to meet your girl friend."

"Yeah, she enjoyed meeting you too," Matt said.

"Could we get back to this? Miss McClure was going to tell me what she saw and heard after you went to sleep," Thorn said.

Matt thought "You did just go to sleep?" was on his mind but Thorn didn't ask the question.

"I woke up after a while. Sometimes I do that and the only thing to do is to get up and read or walk until I feel tired and go back to bed," Peggy said.

"What time was that?" Thorn asked.

"I don't know. The battery was out on my watch so I couldn't tell," Peggy said.

"Was the fire going?" Thorn asked.

"No, only some coals," Peggy said.

"So where did you walk?" Thorn asked.

"I walked down to the shoreline, stood around there for a few minutes. Listened to the lapping of the waves then went back and crawled into bed," Peggy said.

"Did you see anyone else down there?" Thorn said.

"No. It was pretty dark," Peggy said.

"You didn't hear anyone else?" Thorn asked.

"No. Very quiet."

"One other point, Miss McClure. You're an insurance investigator?" Thorn asked.

"Yes."

"You are here investigating a claim that was on the life of Devin Ashton?"

"Yes."

"Miss McClure. That's a lie. I checked with your employer. You are on a leave of absence. They had no idea that you were here in Arizona. Why did you lie, Miss McClure?" Thorn asked.

Peggy looked stricken. "I wanted to prove that Clarisa Ashton was a murderer. She killed my uncle, and I know she killed Devin Ashton as well. My uncle had told us about his affair with Clarisa. He saw what kind of person she really was. I think he even had figured out that she had killed her first husband. My uncle was like a father to me. My own father was killed in Vietnam. When I found out about her husband's death I knew I had to get some closure on this," Peggy said.

"Did you hate Mrs. Montana enough to kill her?" Thorn asked quietly.

"No. Well, yes I might have but I didn't. I was a cop. I work within the law, not outside," Peggy said.

Thorn reached down beside his chair and pulled the envelope with the wrench in it and set it down on the table.

"Have you ever seen this wrench, Miss McClure?" Thorn asked.

Peggy looked at the wrench. "No. I haven't seen one like that since I've been in Arizona," Peggy said.

"OK. That's all I have for now. I think we will wind this up in a day or two," Thorn said.

Peggy stood up, smiled at Matt. "Goodbye, Matt."

"Goodbye, Peggy," Matt said.

When she had gone Thorn said, "She seems to be eyeing you up, Dawson. More went on out there than has been said, didn't it?"

"Now Commander, is that germane to the case? No, she's trying to give me problem with my friend Quincey."

"What it must be like to have the girls falling all over you," Thorn said.

"Oh, would that were true," Matt said.

When Matt and Thorn returned to Thorn's office he had a call waiting from Nick Mautely.

"Yes sir. Almost everything we have was in that preliminary report. We are checking on the wrench, to see if it came along with the purchase of the boat. It's a common wrench, sold by Sears among others," Thorn said.

"Yes, I heard that Montana had moved some of the money out of the country. No, I don't know how much it was," Thorn said.

"It was over twenty million," Matt said.

"Over twenty million," Thorn said into the phone.

"Don't you think that is premature?" Thorn said.

"Yes sir. I agree," Thorn said.

"Alright, you'll be the first one I call," Thorn said and hung up.

"What was that all about?" Matt asked.

"Mautely has gotten the case to the grand jury. He wants to arrest Montana."

"What do you think?" Matt asked.

"Almost everyone on that camping trip had a motive to kill the woman. I think the press has got wind of the money angle and it's putting pressure on Mautely. We need some direct evidence to tie this all down. Who would be your pick?" Thorn asked.

"I'll have to agree that Woody might be the most desperate," Matt said.

Thorn got another call.

"Thorn."

After a few seconds, he said, "OK. Good work. Get a signed statement."

He hung up the phone. "That wrench came with the boat. The boat was a demonstrator so the boat dealer threw in the tool box."

"So Woody owned the wrench. It doesn't mean he was the one to use it," Matt said.

"No. But it seems like he had the strongest motive," Thorn said.

Thorn looked at his watch. "Oh, I'm late for the meeting with the Sheriff. Let's pick this up tomorrow, Matt," Thorn said.

"Yes sir, see you tomorrow."

As Matt drove back to his hotel, he wondered if Woody Montana was guilty. Thinking back to the evening before Clarisa died, Woody did seem fed up with Clarisa. Nothing said, but down there, somewhere in his expression was the beginning of the same loathing that he, Peggy and probably Aaron felt for the woman. Her brother didn't seem to like her that much either and certainly Jenny Paladora might have been seeing her in a different light. Cases weren't made on feelings though, there had to be something that would pinpoint the killer. One more little fact that would clear it all up was needed. Or was that only on TV and the movies, this was real life and it wasn't always that neat. Maybe it was Woody. This is what he had planned from the moment he met Clarisa. Tomorrow was time enough to worry about it.

Twenty Three

Quincey looked over at Matt. He was making so much noise stirring his coffee.

She wasn't sure it was the noise or that he put sugar in his coffee and she couldn't.

She had basically starved herself for over a decade. Get fat and you were out of the

TV anchor business.

Matt glanced up. They were having breakfast in the hotel coffee shop.

"What's wrong?"

"Oh, nothing. What are you going to do today?" Quincey asked.

"I've got a tennis date with Frank over at the Biltmore and then I'm going back

down to the Sheriff's office again. How about you?"

"I'm doing another report from in front of Mr. Montana's home. The buffalo

statues make a nice background. Running low on new information though. Can't

you give me a little something?"

"I think the county attorney is going to the grand jury," Matt said.

"Really, who does he think did this?"

"You'll have to get that from him," Matt said.

"Well, that's something, I've got to go. Please call me on your cell phone if you

hear something," Quincey said.

"Sure," Matt said and he gave her a quick kiss.

Matt found Frank setting in the shade by the Biltmore tennis courts talking to an

attractive lady. As Matt approached she got up and went inside the pro shop.

"How's it going? Make a new friend?" Matt asked as he sat down beside Frank.

"We were warming up before you came. I guess her husband was called away to

the phone and hadn't come back so we hit the ball around," Frank said.

"Oh, oh, unfair advantage, you're all warmed up," Matt said.

"You can warm up as long as you like."

"Any progress finding the fisherman?" Matt asked.

"Maybe. I talked to one clerk who thought that the fellow in question should be out there, at the lake, buying bait this evening about eight," Frank said.

"Good. He might have the little bit of information we need to tie this down," Matt said.

"Want to go flying later today?" Frank asked.

"I need to get down to the Sheriff's office when we finish," Matt said.

"I got a call from my friend that lives over in Chandler. He is going to let me take up his Cessna later this morning," Frank said.

"That should be fun. You'll still be able to check out the fisherman?"

"Oh, sure. Probably run up to Sedona and back."

Matt's cell phone rang. It was Quincey.

"Matt, I'm on the freeway heading out of Phoenix. As I pulled up to Mr. Montana's driveway he passed me in a Lexus Sport Utility. I turned around and followed."

"Is he by himself?" Matt asked.

"No, the burly man driving, the one that knocked the microphone out of my hand," Quincey said.

"That would be Dirk Smith," Matt said.

"Didn't the police tell him not to leave town?" Quincey said.

"Yes they did. Hang on. Don't get too close. I'll call Thorn and call you back," Matt said.

"What's up?" Frank asked.

"It looks like Woody might be making a run for it," Matt said. He dialed Thorn's cell phone.

"Thorn."

"Hi. This is Matt Dawson. Woody Montana and probably Dirk Smith are in Montana's sport utility and headed south on the freeway out of town," Matt said.

"How do you know that?"

"My lady friend is tailing them. She went out to his house this morning to do a TV report and they passed her heading south," Matt said.

"Is she still behind them?"

"I think so," Matt said.

"OK. I can have him picked up for questioning. I'll contact the DPS and get them to stop them. I'll get back to you," Thorn said.

"Where are they?" Frank asked.

"Headed south on the freeway I guess," Matt said.

"Let's head them off."

"What?"

"I've got a plane rearing to go down at Sky Harbor, let's go," Frank said.

"All right," Matt said. He immediately felt better knowing he could do something, possibly keeping Quincey from getting into trouble.

Frank and Matt ran out of the Biltmore, causing a raised eyebrow or two and went out to Matt's Z3 in the parking lot. Fortunately, a convenient freeway entrance that got them down to Sky Harbor in only a few minutes since they were ahead of the rush hour. Matt was lucky enough not to get a speeding ticket. They found the Cessna and were air born only a half-hour after Matt had made the call to Thorn.

Matt called Quincey back as Frank banked the plane south toward the freeway down to Tucson.

"Yeah," Quincey said.

"Are they still in sight?" Matt asked.

"Yes, they are several cars and trucks ahead. The freeway is crowded and they really can't get too far ahead," Quincey said.

"Where are you now?"

"We're coming up an intersection with another freeway. US 8 which goes to Yuma," Quincey said.

"OK. We're in a light plane and we should be over you in a few minutes," Matt said.

Matt called Thorn.

"Thorn."

"It's Matt Dawson, again. My friend happened to have a light plane ready to go so we're in the air, over the freeway headed down to Tucson. I talked to Quincey. She still has them in sight, she's crossing the intersection with I8 right now," Matt said.

"You're breaking up, but I got most of that. I talked to Mautely and we've got our warrant. I'll contact the DPS again. See if you can get eye contact," Thorn said.

"Understood. I'll call again if anything changes," Matt said.

Matt picked them up a small pair of binoculars under the dash studied the traffic on the freeway.

Matt phone rang again.

"Matt it's Quincey. I see a roadblock about a mile or so up the freeway. Wait. Montana sees it too he's slowing down and pulling over to the shoulder. I'm going to stop too."

"Qunicey, be careful," Matt said. Up ahead to the right of the freeway was a small desert mountain and at the exit to the left of the mountain Matt could see the Department of Public Safety roadblock.

"I think that's Picacho Peak," Frank said.

"There they are," Matt said. The Lexus Sport Utility had pulled off the freeway to the right. Quincey's rented sedan was another hundred yards in back of the Lexus.

Frank banked the Cessna to circle the cars below.

"Quincey, are you by yourself?" Matt asked.

"No. I've got Hime, my cameraman with me. Matt, they're pulling off the road. There's no exit but they're heading off across the desert," Qunicey said.

Matt leaned over and saw the Lexus bouncing across the desert heading for a dried up streambed. He looked back to the freeway. Quincey was following with her rented sedan.

"Quincey, what are you doing? You're supposed to report the news, not make it," Matt said.

Matt hung up the phone and dialed Thorn.

"Thorn."

"It's me again. I have a situation. Montana saw the roadblock at the mountain exit, Picacho Peak. He's taken off across the desert to the west in his SUV. Unfortunately, Quincey is following him."

"What? Hang on and I'll get in contact with DPS," Thorn said.

Frank passed over the two cars struggling across the desert, throwing up considerable dust clouds and bumping around severely. Quincey's sedan came to a stop, having run up on a boulder and steam was coming out of the car's hood. The SUV had made it to the streambed and was tearing down the wash.

"Here comes the cavalry," Frank said.

Matt looked back toward the freeway as two DPS off road vehicles tore across the desert. One of the units stopped by Quincey's car. She stood by the car with her hands on her hips. The other continued on to the wash. Frank circled again and headed down the wash. The Lexus had come to a small bridge. As Matt watched it pulled up the side of the streambed and onto a dirt road and headed west.

"Thorn, are you there?"

"Yeah, I'm in contact with the DPS officers out there," Thorn said.

"They pulled out of the streambed they were in and up on a dirt road heading out west," Matt said.

"Right, I'll relay that," Thorn said.

As they flew down over the road the Lexus had taken Matt noticed two highway patrol cars on a paved road to the south of their position. The dirt road turned northwest and the Lexus threw up a cloud of dust that could be seen for miles. As Frank completed yet another circle the dirt road ran into an intersection with the paved road. The two DPS cars formed a roadblock at the intersection. Matt could see the officers out of the car, pistols drawn, hanging over the hoods of their cars. The Lexus came to a stop. Woody and Dirk Smith got out of the car with their hands up.

"Well, that ends that," Frank said.

"Yeah, nothing says I'm guilty like running from the law," Matt said.

"Unless, of course, you're OJ," Frank said.

"Quincy is going to be burned that she wasn't there for the finish," Matt said.

Frank turned the plane back north and set a course for Sky Harbor.

At three o'clock that afternoon Rick Mautely held his new conference. Quincey and her cameraman barely made it back to the Maricopa County Court building in yet another rental car. She pushed her way up to the front and was ready to go with questions even if she was dirty and dusty. Matt and Thorn were asked to be present in case any questions came up that Mautely needed backup on.

"This morning the Department of Public Safety apprehended Mr. Wodrow Montana and his employee Mr. Dirk Smith while presumably attempting to flee into Mexico. They were arrested after a chase across the desert near Picacho Peak off the freeway down to Tuscon. Mr. Montana is charged with first-degree murder of his wife, the former Mrs. Clarisa Ashton of San Francisco. Mr. Smith is charged with aiding criminal flight. We believe Mr. Montana killed his wife for financial reasons

and look forward to a swift prosecution in this case. Are there any questions?"
Mautely asked.

"Has Mr. Montana been released on bail?" the New Republic reporter asked.

"No. Since there was an attempt to flee the judge ruled there was to be no bail,"
Mautely said.

"Do you have any direct evidence that Montana killed his wife?" Quincey asked.

"I can't go into any details of the case at this point," Matuely said.

"How will this affect the 200 million dollar fortune?" the AP reporter asked.

"That is not a matter for my office. I understand there are others who will be
litigating that question."

"Will you ask for the death penalty?" the Arizona Republic reporter asked.

"That is a question to be asked at a later date and only if we are successful in
prosecuting Mr. Montana," Mautely said.

"Do you credit the Sheriff's Office with the arrest in this case?" the channel five
reporters asked.

"The Department of Public Safety is to be commended for the way they took
these two men into custody without anyone being hurt," Mautely said.

"We were just standing around with our thumbs up our butts," Thorn muttered to
Matt.

Twenty Four

The next morning Matt stared out the window at the mountains to the east with the sun coming out over the red tiled roofs interspersed with various sized palm trees. It was going to be another beautiful day in the Valley of the Sun, not a cloud in sight. He was waiting for Quincey to get ready to go down for breakfast. She was in a bad mood slamming things around. No wonder, she found out she was going to have to pay to have the first rental car repaired. She felt that they would have covered it all if she had got the pictures of Woody being taken into custody. Matt hadn't slept well himself. Somewhere down deep he felt something was wrong. Something didn't fit. Maybe he was just hungry.

Matt's cell phone rang. It was Conway Santell, Woody's attorney.

"Yes, Mr. Santell, what can I do for you?" Matt asked.

"Woody would like to talk to you. Will you go down and see him?" Santell asked.

"I don't know what good that would do," Matt said.

"Frankly, I don't either, but he would really like to talk to you for a short time. I would think you might be curious as to what he has to say," Santell said.

"I guess I would be."

"Fine. He's at the Madison Street jail at the moment. I know he'll appreciate seeing you," Santell said and he disconnected.

After breakfast with Quincey, Matt headed down to the Madison Street jail complex. This was an actual brick and mortar facility, since Woody was accused of murder he wasn't put in the Tent City jail.

When Woody sat down opposite of Matt he looked tired and frightened.

"Thanks for coming down, Matt," Woody said.

"I was curious to hear what you have to say," Matt said.

"I want you to help me," Woody said.

"How could I do that?"

"Find out who killed Clarisa," Woody said.

"They're pretty sure you did it, Woody," Matt said.

"That's just it. I didn't kill her. I knew they were going to pin this on me. That's why I ran. Matt, I didn't do it. I think you can help me."

"Why is that?"

"You know that several other people at that campsite that hated her. If your report is to be believed, her own brother might have done it. She was drunk that night. She was saying things that hurt people. I know her brother was angry. They both had a big row I haven't told anyone about just before we headed out to the lake," Woody said.

"Woody, I'm going to tell you straight. For some reason I kind of like you, but there's one thing that really hangs me up. I find it hard to believe you. You don't always tell the truth," Matt said.

"About what?"

"Not knowing Claris was filthy rich for instance," Matt said.

Woody looked down at his hands and said,"Alright. You're right. I knew she was rich as sin. I did some investigating when I realized she was something out of the ordinary. I was in some financial trouble so I married her. I was fond of her though, but as time went on, she became harder and harder to deal with. But I'm not a murderer. I didn't kill her. Hell, if I was going to do that I would have done it some other way. Not with all these witnesses around."

Matt shook his head and looked away. He seemed to be telling the truth.

"Matt, I'll pay you."

"That's not a problem. I've already got a client who just wants the truth. What do you want me to do?" Matt asked. Carson Aston's truth might be different than Woody's.

"Find out who killed her. Believe me. I didn't do it. Someone else did. Find out who," Woody said.

"I can't promise anything, but I'll see what I can do," Matt said.

"Thanks. Get me out of this and I'll fix you up with buffalo steaks for life," Woody said.

I'm too easy, Matt thought to himself as he headed back out to the parking lot.

Matt made one more trip out to Thorn's office. He knocked on the open door as Thorn had his nose down in a stack of paper work.

"Oh, hi, Dawson, come on in."

"I just got back from talking to Woody Montana," Matt said.

"Oh, yeah, what did he say?"

"He didn't do it," Matt said.

Thorn laughed.

"He might be telling the truth," Matt said.

"Matt, only a rare few people we arrest that admit to their crimes," Thorn said.

"I know and he ran. He said he thought he was going to be arrested so he got frightened and decided to run," Matt said.

"You believe he is innocent?"

"Not necessarily, but several other people there had motives as well, and he made one good point."

"What was that?"

"If he was going to kill her, he wouldn't do it with all those people around."

"That might be the perfect time, other people there with motives. People might think someone else did it just as you are doing now," Thorn said.

"You said it. There is reasonable doubt," Matt said.

Thorn put down his stack of papers, leaned back in his chair and took off his glasses. He rubbed his eyes.

"What else should we do to prove this to your satisfaction?" Thorn said.

"I think we should keep poking around for a while longer. You could use something else for your case against Woody anyway," Matt said.

Thorn's phone rang.

"Thorn."

He covered the mouthpiece and turned to Matt. "There is a Mr. Frank Pullen here, looking for you."

"He's my partner, sort of."

"Show him back to my office, please," Thorn said into the phone.

In a few minutes Frank appeared at the door with a wide-bodied figure in tow.

Matt got up and moved to the door. "Hi, Frank. Deputy Thorn, this is my friend Frank Pullen. Frank, this is the Commander of the General Investigation, Tom Thorn."

Thorn got up and came around the desk and extended his hand to Frank.

"Nice to meet you, Commander Thorn. Frank Pullen. This is Luke Dillard. He is one of the fishermen that were out at Lake Pleasant the night Clarisa Ashton was killed," Frank said.

"Let's step across to the conference room, it would be crowded if we tried to sit down in here," Thorn said.

Thorn led the parade down the hall to the next available conference room. Matt followed Luke Dillard as he walked ponderously down the hall. Luke had on a baseball cap, a dingy T-shirt straining to cover the overlap his belly made at his belt line. The T-shirt was decorated with a 'Lake Mead Bass Tournament of eighty-nine' logo. He had on dirty blue jeans and wore workman's boots and looked to have a several day beard over his pudgy face.

They all settled around the conference table after Frank moved a couple of chairs back to give Luke more room.

"How did you find Mr. Dillard, Mr. Pullen?" Thorn asked.

"Call me Frank. I spent time out at the lake's best bait shop. One of the clerks thought that Mr. Dillard here might well have been at the lake that evening. He didn't know his name but said he came out regularly the same evening each week, so I went out that night and waited until he came in," Frank said.

"Good work, Frank. Now Mr.Dillard, were you at the lake on the evening that Mrs. Montana was killed?" Thorn asked.

"Yes, sir. I remember reading about it the next day or so," Dillard said.

"You go out to fish at night?" Thorn asked.

"Yep. Me and Carl go out once a week in my little bass boat, all during the season, except during December and January, of course. It's a mite cold then," Dillard said.

"Carl?" Thorn asked.

"Yeah. Carl Spense, he works at a station over in Wickenburg. We went to high school together. Carl and I been fishing over thirty years."

"I see. So what part of the lake were you on that night?" Thorn said.

"Carl and me could never decide on which was the best spot so we have route we take each evenin. We go up to the west shore, a little more than halfway up. We troll around the lake heading north and then around back down toward the dam," Dillard said.

"You just kept moving?" Thorn asked.

"Yeah. We go in and around all the larger coves and little bays and such. We stay, oh, twenty yards off shore. We usually find one spot or another where they're bitin, and then we'll stay in one spot for a while," Dillard said.

"Do you know which cove it was that the Montana's had their camp?" Thorn said.

"Yeah, Frank and I went on up there in my boat that evening he came looking for me. I remember that night we didn't find any spot too good so we kept movin," Dillard said.

"Do you remember anything when you were going by the campsite?" Thorn asked.

"Well, yes a little, not much," Dillard said.

"And what was that?" Thorn asked.

"It was real dark that night, only starlight. We came into that little cove and went around it kinda clock wise, not too far off shore. My little trolling motor is real quite so we could hear pretty good. Two people were sitting down by the water, talkin. Drinking I think. Looked like a fire up behind them but it was just coals. One of the two people was real loud. Like she was drunk or somethin. Laughing, cackalin really. You hear a lot of drunk people out at campsites late at night so we didn't think a whole lot about it," Dillard said.

"The loudest one was a woman?" Thorn asked.

"Yep. Pretty sure about that," Dillard said.

"How about the other one. What can you tell us about the other person?"

Dillard closed his eyes and squinted.

"Not much really. Both of them were just sittin there. I think I saw a bottle in the hands of the loud one."

"Could you hear what she was saying?" Matt asked.

"Naw. Wasn't listening really."

"Tell them how come you remember all this," Frank said.

"Oh, yeah. When Frank here was asking about this, what brought it to mind was the power boat," Dillard said.

"What about the power boat?" Thorn asked.

"Well, it was a little off shore. Almost ran into the darn thing. Maybe lookin in on the two people on the shore diverted my attention or something but I looked up at the last second and this thing maybe twenty yards or so off shore was right in front of us. Had to throw the helm over and push off the darn thing. We bumped it but I don't think there was a scratch or anything," Dillard said.

"Was the boat drifting?" Matt said.

"Yeah, it could have been."

Thorn asked Dillard about the pair on the shore several different ways but he couldn't add anything else.

"Thanks, Mr. Dillard, you can go now. I really appreciate you coming in," Thorn said.

"Sure. Glad to help. Is there any reward money?" Dillard said.

"No. Not that I know of. Be sure my secretary has your name and number. Thanks again," Thorn said.

"Sure. Glad to help," Dillard said again a left managing to just get through the door without turning sideways.

Thorn leaned over the table finishing up his notes on his yellow pad. Frank turned to Matt.

"So is this wrapped up, you're sure Montana did it?" Frank said.

Thorn looked up. "Not according to Dawson here, he got a news flash, Montana says he didn't do it," he said and laughed.

"Montana asked me to go down and see him at the jail. He says he wouldn't be so stupid as to do it around so many people," Matt said.

"I say he did it then because there were other people to blame on the scene," Thorn said.

"By the way, Montana did admit that he knew Clarisa was rich before he married her," Matt said.

"Just enough truth to sucker you in," Thorn said.

"At least four other people in the group who had cause to think Clarisa was better off dead," Frank said.

"Mr. Montana had the most number of reasons, two hundred million of them," Thorn said.

"How would you feel when you find out that someone you are living with probably killed your mother?" Matt said.

"Aaron had the same opportunity to kill her that Woody did," Frank said.

"Another 'by the way'. Woody said that Clarisa and her brother, David Wilkes, had a terrible argument just before they all left on the camping trip," Matt said.

"How convenient. As long as we are bringing up other people, your girl friend, Peggy McClure was quite emotional about Clarisa, enough so to come down here to Arizona on her own time and money to see if she could get her," Thorn said.

"Have you got that autopsy report with you?" Matt asked.

"On Clarisa? Yeah, I think I do." Thorn shuffled down through a folder of papers he had laying on the table in front of him.

Matt read through the report again.

"That lawyer lady also had some reasons to hate Clarisa, though they were from long ago," Frank said.

"What was the deal with her?" Thorn asked.

"Clarisa probably killed her high school boy friend of the time, a Bobby Bennington. That's where Clarisa first got her taste of running people down with cars," Frank said.

"Tom, let's get all these people together for one more question and answer session," Matt said.

"What, you mean like in some Charlie Chan movie?" Thorn asked.

"I guess. Only, I don't have anyone else picked as yet," Matt said.

"Maricopa County has already picked Mr. Woody Montana," Thorn said.

"Three of the four are staying at Woody's place, we could easily get them together there," Matt said.

"What would you ask them that you haven't already asked?" Frank asked.

"I don't know for sure, maybe something will come out of jogging their collective minds," Matt said.

"I suppose it couldn't hurt. Now that Woody is in jail maybe they will say something they might not have before," Thorn said.

Twenty Five

Thorn set the meeting up for the next morning at ten. He had managed to reach all four of the former campers. Wilkes was the most angry and uncooperative saying that he needed to get back to his business but he had finally agreed to the meeting. Aaron Ashton was also upset at the need for further interview by the Sheriff's Office but also agreed to the meeting. Both Peggy McClure and Jenny Paladora had no comment on being asked to come to another interview.

Thorn had stopped by Matt's hotel to pick him up which would save him a great deal of unnecessary driving. Thorn drove his unmarked car up the driveway past the buffalo statues and parked under an entry roof. Glancing out into the large animal pen, Matt saw four buffalo spending the morning under their shade covering. He and Thorn got out of the car and went up the stone walkway, which led to Woody Montana's front door. They were met with an angry glare from Dirk Smith who answered the doorbell.

"Hi, Dirk," Matt said.

Smith only grunted in return. Matt and Thorn moved on into the entry hall. Peggy McClure was sitting on a small bench in the entry hall. She stood and stretched her back.

"That thing is for looks, not sitting," Peggy said.

"Hi, Peggy, besides your back, how are you?" Matt asked.

"Great, but Deputy Thorn, I need to get back to work. Will this be the final meeting?" Peggy asked.

"I think so, we need to clear up a few details," Thorn said.

"Dirk's out on bail?" Matt whispered to Thorn.

"No, they dropped the charges, the judge felt that when he started driving Montana, there was no warrant for Montana's arrest," Thorn said.

David Wilkes came down the hallway.

"Let's get this over with. I've already canceled two flights back to Wyoming. We can meet in here," Wilkes said. He moved off to his right into a western motif dinning room.

The dinning room contained a large Spanish style table and eight straight backed chairs. On the walls several of the western paintings that Matt thought he had seen before in Clarisa's San Francisco home. Woody's addition had to be the buffalo head hanging over the chair at the head of the table.

David Wilkes took that chair, apparently now the man in charge. Matt and Thorn sat on one side and Peggy McClure sat down across from Matt. Jenny Paladora came into the dinning room and Matt and Thorn stood up.

"Jenny, is Aaron coming? You wanted him in on the meeting as well, didn't you Deputy?" Wilkes asked Thorn.

"Yes, I did," Thorn said.

"I'll see if I can find him," Jenny said and she went back down the hall.

"You have Montana in jail awaiting trial. Why is it necessary for us to still be here in Arizona?" Wilkes asked.

"A few more points to clear up," Thorn said.

Wilkes was still thinking of some response when Aaron came into the dinning followed closely by Jenny Paladora.

Matt noticed Jenny Paladora looked tired, as if she hadn't been sleeping lately. Aaron seemed nervous and had trouble pulling out a chair beside David Wilkes.

"These are the most uncomfortable dam chairs," Aaron said.

"I'll try to make this brief as possible," Thorn said. The chairs were very uncomfortable.

"What else could you possible have to ask us?" Wilkes asked.

"First of all, I'd like to ask you if you have anything else to add. We have arrested Mr. Montana for the crime. Did any of you see or hear anything which would bear on the guilt or innocence of Mr. Montana?" Thorn asked.

After a period of silence Aaron said, "I'm not sure that there is anyone here that was that sorry to see her dead."

"Does that include you Mr. Wilkes? Clarisa was your sister," Thorn asked.

"Certainly not. I loved my sister in my own way. She had a long and fortunate life. If Woody killed her, he should pay the price," Wilkes said.

"Do you think he killed her? Did you hear or see anything which would indicate that?" Thorn said.

"I think he needed money, and as it stands he will be a rich man now," Wilkes said.

"Maybe," Thorn said.

"Montana says that you and Clarisa had a serious fight about financial matters just before you all left on the camping trip. Is that true, Mr. Wilkes?" Matt asked.

"I'll say, they were screaming at each other. Why is it that you thought Clarisa owed you so much, David?" Aaron asked.

Wilkes only glared at Aaron in response.

"Yes, we did have a disagreement about the timing of her investment in my company's stock offering, but, I didn't kill her," Wilkes said.

"No one accused you of that Mr. Wilkes. Let's move on. We now have a witness that says he saw two people sitting down by the water's edge, after everyone else had gone to bed. Sitting and talking and probably sharing a bottle. One of these people was Clarisa. Which one of you was the other?" Thorn asked.

Matt glanced from face to face, trying to see if there would be any reaction that would give one of them away. Wilkes seemed shocked and troubled. Aaron seemed his usual angry self. Peggy McClure seemed excited and was glancing at the other's reactions as well. Jenny Paladora seemed shocked and stared out across the table at a point on the wall.

"Mr. Wilkes, were you the one sitting down at the water's edge that night?" Thorn asked.

"No. Definitely not," Wilkes said.

"Mr. Aston?" Thorn asked.

"Not me. I was asleep."

"Miss McClure?"

"No sir," Peggy asked.

"Miss Paladora?" Thorn asked.

Jenny Paladora simply shook her head.

"I'm wondering if you all would take a like detector test on this point?" Thorn asked.

No one volunteered.

"Matt, you had something you wanted to ask?" Thorn said.

"Yes, thanks Commander. Could I have the wrench?" Matt asked.

Thorn reached down to his briefcase, opened it up and took out the wrench, which was in a plastic bag and sported a bright yellow evidence tag. Matt stood up and came around behind Thorn and took the wrench.

"This is the wrench we believe killed Mrs. Montana. I'd like each of you to carefully look at the wrench. Examine it up closely and tell me if you could testify that this was in fact the wrench that was on the boat," Matt said.

"Could you check it first Mr. Wilkes," Matt said and handed it to David Wilkes.

Wilkes took the wrench in his right hand and examined it closely.

"Yes, I think that was the one Woody used to fix the motor problem," Wilkes said.

Matt took back the wrench and moved over off behind the right shoulder of Aaron Ashton.

"What do you think, Aaron?" Matt asked.

Aaron turned slightly toward Matt, and reached up and took the wrench. He turned it over several times and handed it back.

"Yeah, that's the one."

Matt moved over off to the right should of Peggy McClure. She partially turned and took the wrench. She brought the wrench up close to her face and carefully looked at the tool as if expecting to see some bloodstains.

"I never saw this before you showed it to me once before," Peggy said.

Matt took the wrench back and moved over to Jenny Paladora's right shoulder.

"I don't see what this is accomplishing," Jenny said.

"Take a careful look at it, Miss Paladora," Thorn said.

Jenny pushed her chair back and pulled it around to face Matt. She reached up and took the wrench with her left hand. Her lip quivered and she put the wrench in her lap.

"What do you think, Miss Paladora?" Matt asked.

She only shook her head.

"You've seen that wrench before haven't you Miss Paladora?" Matt asked.

Jenny still didn't respond.

"It's the one you used to hit Clarisa, isn't it Miss Paladora? Why did you do that?"

"No, it wasn't me," Jenny finally said, crying.

"Jenny, you are a lawyer. You know we have you. The blows to Clarisa Ashton's head were on the upper right side on the top of her head from someone that was facing her. A left-handed person inflicted that wound. Miss Paladora, you were the only one that took the wrench in your left hand," Matt said.

"How do you know that Woody isn't left handed?" Peggy McClure asked.

"When we had scuffle out front here, I remember Woody picking things up with his right hand," Matt said.

"How about it? Why don't you tell us what happened that night, Jenny. I don't think you're the kind of person that could live with this. Woody Montana didn't do it, did he?" Matt asked.

Jenny struggled with herself for a few seconds.

"No... Yes, I did it. She was a monster. She deserved to die," Jenny let out in a burst of emotion.

"Did you plan to kill her?" Thorn asked.

"No. No, no."

"What happened Jenny?" Matt asked.

"We were sitting down at the shore, after everyone else had gone to sleep. I couldn't get to sleep so I went outside and she saw me and waved me to come down to the campfire. We moved down to the water's edge. She was drinking and talking. Bragging about all the 'buffaloes' she had killed. 'Just takes the guts to do it' she said. It was then she told me about her first one. Bobby Bennington. She was too drunk to remember how I felt about Bobby. He was the love of my life. She said he was the perfect catch. She went all the way with him, got pregnant and wanted Bobby to marry her. The bastard 'wouldn't marry white trash' is what he told her. Told her to get an abortion."

"Did she say how she killed him?" Matt asked.

"Yeah, she was really up and wanted to tell me how clever she had been. She remembered that the pastor that had those parties for us teenagers always kept the keys in his car. She went over to his house, the garage was open and she stole the car right out in broad daylight. She had seen Bobby Bennington earlier so she waited until he was trying to cross the street, she gunned it and killed him," Jenny said.

"She told you all this?" Matt asked.

"Yeah, she was really proud of it. Said it took great amounts of courage. That I should turn my life around too, just get what I want, eliminate anyone in my way," Jenny said.

"Is that when you killed her?" Thorn asked.

"No, I was shocked and angry. I couldn't say anything. She saw that the powerboat was floating away. She stood up, and staggered out into the water. She started swimming toward the boat. She was having trouble swimming so I took off my blouse and went in after her. She was floundering but had almost made it to the boat. I swam up to the boat and got up on the stern and was trying to grab her and pull her in when she said one thing too many," Peggy said.

"What did she say?" Matt asked.

"She said 'Pull me up, you stupid bitch'. It was too much. She had killed Bobby Bennington, the only man I've ever truly loved. The wrench was lying there on the boat floor. I picked it up."

"You hit her?" Matt asked softly.

"Yes, yes…she ruined my life, she was a monster," Jenny cried.

They all sat there staring at Jenny who was bent over crying into her lap.

"She should get a medal," Aaron said.

"It doesn't work that way," Thorn said quietly.

Thorn came around and put the cuffs on Jenny and led her from the room.

Everyone seemed too shocked to say anything. Peggy and Aaron moved out to the hallway.

"David, could I ask you a question?" Matt asked.

"What? I had no idea of what Jenny had done," Wilkes said.

"I know. Why did you think Clarisa owed you so much?"

"That was a long time ago. It don't see why it matters now."

"If it was a long time ago then the statues of limitations surely would cover anything you did that was a crime," Matt said.

"I'll tell you but only if you promise not to repeat it," Wilkes said.

"OK. The case is over now," Matt said.

"Clarisa did kill Bobby Bennington. He got her pregnant, refused to do the honorable thing. She got an abortion at his insistence. So she stole a car and killed him. I came home one afternoon to find her crying in the living room. She told me what she had done. She was not thinking of trying to get away with it. She had parked the car she used out in a vacant lot behind our house. I went out and took the car down to the local swampy area and ran it into the water. They didn't find the thing until years later," Wilkes said.

"You started her on her lifetime career of serial murders," Matt said and turned

away.

McDaniel/ONE TOO MANY BUFFALOES

Twenty Six

The little blue Z3 tore down the highway across southwestern Arizona. Matt and Quincey had an early start for the six-hour drive home to San Diego. Out in the distance dark green fields were in sharp contrast to the desert mountains and hills closer to the highway.

Quincey was drowsy, not used to being up at the hour.

"What's all that green?" Quincey asked.

"Probably lettuce. This is a big lettuce growing area," Matt said.

"Are you glad that this whole thing is over?" Quincey asked.

"Yeah. The saga of Clarisa is frightening in a way. How could she get away with murder for so many years?"

"If it were not for the huge fortune involved she might have. Has the money thing been resolved?"

"Yes. Carson and Woody made a deal and the bulk of the money went back to the heirs in the original will."

"Then the hospital got the lion share?" Quincey asked.

"Yes. That's one good thing out of all this," Matt said.

"Thanks for getting me that interview with Woody," Quincey said.

"Did the networks like that one?"

"I guess. It made three out of their five prime time news shows. It paid off for me too," Quincey said.

"How's that?"

"They decided now to pick up all my car bills."

"That's great," Matt said.

"You know Clarisa had the most perverted philosophy of life. Just taking only what she needed. That is, needed to be filthy rich," Quincey said.

Matt stretched his arms. "I guess she killed one too many buffaloes."